MURDER IN PASTICHE

OR NINE DETECTIVES ALL AT SEA

MARION MAINWARING

PANDORA

London

MURDER IN PASTICHE

OR NINE DETECTIVES ALL AT SEA

MARION MAINWARING

London

This edition first published in Great Britain in 1987 by
Pandora Press (Routledge & Kegan Paul Ltd)
11 New Fetter Lane, London EC4P 4EE

Set in Linotron Sabon 10/11pt
by Input Typesetting Ltd, London SW19 8DR printed in Great Britain
by Cox & Wyman Ltd, Reading

British Library Cataloguing in Publication Data

Mainwaring, Marion
Murder in pastiche, or, Nine detectives
all at sea.—(Pandora women crime writers)
I. Title
823'.914[F]   PR6063.A34/

ISBN 0–86358–206–0

Pandora Women Crime Writers

Series Editors: Rosalind Coward and Linda Semple

In introducing the *Pandora Women Crime Writers* series we have two aims: to reprint the best of women crime writers who have disappeared from print and to introduce a new generation of women crime writers to all devotees of the genre. We also hope to seduce new readers to the pleasures of detective fiction.

Women have used the tradition of crime writing inventively since the end of the last century. Indeed in many periods women have dominated crime writing, as in the so-called Golden Age of Detective fiction, usually defined as between the first novel of Agatha Christie and the last of Dorothy L. Sayers. Often the most popular novels of the day, and those thought to be the best in their genre, were written by women. But as in so many areas of women's writing, many of these have been allowed to go out of print. Few people know the names of Josephine Bell, Pamela Branch, Hilda Lawrence, Marion Mainwaring or Anthony Gilbert (whose real name was Lucy Malleson). Their novels are just as good and entertaining as when they were first written.

Women's importance in the field of crime writing is just as vital today. P. D. James, Ruth Rendell and Patricia Highsmith have all ensured that crime writing is treated seriously. Not so well known, but equally flourishing, is a new branch of feminist crime writers. We plan to introduce many new writers from this area, from England and other countries.

The integration of reprints and new novels is sometimes uneasy. Some writers do make snobbish, even racist remarks. However it is a popular misconception that all earlier novels are always snobbish and racist. Many of our chosen and favourite authors managed to avoid, sometimes deliberately, the prevailing views. Others are more rooted in the ideologies of the time but when their remarks jar, it does serve to remind us that any novel must be understood by reference to the historical context in which it was written.

Some of the best writers who will be appearing in this series are: Josephine Bell, Ina Bouman, Christianna Brand, Pamela Branch, Sarah Dreher, Katherine V. Forrest, Miles Franklin, Anthony Gilbert (Lucy Malleson), Hilda Lawrence, Marion Mainwaring, Nancy Spain . . .

Linda Semple
Rosalind Coward

The first novels to be published during 1987 are:

Green for Danger by Christianna Brand
Death of a Doll by Hilda Lawrence
Murder in Pastiche by Marion Mainwaring
and
Amateur City by Katherine V. Forrest

Our autumn 1987 titles are:

Bring the Monkey by Miles Franklin
Stoner McTavish by Sarah Dreher
The Port of London Murders by Josephine Bell
The Spinster's Secret by Anthony Gilbert (Lucy Malleson)
Murder at the Nightwood Bar by Katherine V. Forrest

See back of book for selected titles.

PART ONE

CHAPTER 1

PRELUDE IN LIVERPOOL

The captain stroked his forked, wavy beard and gazed out over the foredeck of the R.M.S. *Florabunda;* his wild melancholy greenish eyes seemed to penetrate beyond the ship, beyond the oily waters of the canal, sullied with waste paper and scraps of food, to the Mersey, the Irish Sea, and the broad Atlantic.

'We shall make the tide after all, Mr Waggish,' he said.

A piercing blast from the whistle prevented any answer. The First Officer, a lean man in his late thirties with dark hair, bright blue eyes, and a smooth tanned face, merely nodded.

'And in seven days – ' The Captain left this sentence unfinished. He sighed heavily and looked down at the sailing orders he was holding:

R.M.S. *Florabunda*, Liverpool (Dock 4–b) 3 Oct. 195–*Due* New York (Ruggarty Pier) 10 Oct. *do.*

A ruddy, yellow-haired young man with a Purser's stripes on his sleeve appeared and held out a sheaf of papers. 'The schedule, sir. Passengers all present and accounted for.'

The Captain glared at the papers as if they were unclean. With a prolonged snort, rather like the whistle on a smaller scale, he turned on his heel and stalked out of the wheelhouse.

The Purser shrugged and handed the papers to Mr Waggish.

A chubby man with red and gold stripes on his sleeve, the ship's Doctor, came in from the boat-deck where he had been smoking his pipe and watching the last stages of cargo-

3

loading. 'How *is* the Skipper, anyway?' he asked idly; the Doctor was just returned from three weeks' leave.

'Same as ever, *I* should say,' the First Officer replied indifferently, running his eye down the passenger list. 'Wouldn't *you* say, Tom?'

'No change,' agreed the Purser. Glancing sidelong at the First Officer, he inquired with the caution of one who performs a necessary but slightly perilous social obligation: 'Had you a good holiday, Doctor?'

The Doctor's pudgy face lighted up. 'Oh, aye,' he said eagerly. 'Very fine, thank you. Very successful. My fifth canto is nearly completed. Ah, there's a magnificent bit towards the end.' Taking his pipe from his mouth, he declaimed:

'As when the fierce Hyrcanian Tiger greedy for his prey
Deep-crouchèd in his jungle lair doth milky lambs
    waylay – '

'Oh, damn' good,' said the Purser loudly. 'Yes. Damn good. What – ' But his words were lost in the flow of the Doctor's recitation:

'As when the vengeful Lion wild with elemental rage
Doth Elephant or Crocodile in gory duel engage –
As when the savage ebon Pard aflame at sight of foe
Doth pounce upon the Billy-goat, or tender Buffalow –
So Tipptop with his flashing sword at Sarcino came,
His wrongs t'avenge, and publicize the fair Gazella's name!'

The Doctor delivered this remarkable passage with his eyes closed, making little jabbing motions with his pipe; as his ardour grew, so did his Tyneside accent. 'You must hear it all,' he said. 'Perhaps *this* trip you'll have time.' He looked at the Purser wistfully: his last suggestion appeared to be based on optimism rather than experience.

'Oh, definitely, one day, if only there's time,' the Purser said politely. 'Or the First will listen to you, he's more of a literary bloke than I am, you know. Eh, Waggish?'

The First Officer did not answer; he was still scanning the schedule.

'Some promising material,' the Purser observed, nodding

towards the list of passengers. 'There's a Yankee blonde who looks like a film actress. There's a *very* pretty little dark-haired girl. There's a number of real celebrities – '

'Good heavens!' Mr Waggish interrupted. His eyes were round in his dark, suave face. 'Look here!'

The others followed his finger down the columns of names; it tapped nine times.

'Aye?' The Doctor's face was blank.

'Look, you clot!' said the First Officer vehemently. He pointed to the names again.

'I thought you'd be interested,' said the Purser.

'Some of them do sound familiar.' The Doctor spoke rather doubtfully. 'Isn't that Lord Simon Quinsey the famous detective – '

'Familiar! And you call yourself a literary man!' began the First Officer, with some scorn; but before he could continue, he started and looked at his watch. 'I shall be late,' he said. Tossing the papers back to the Purser, he hurried off toward the bow.

The names he had indicated were:

> Mr Trajan Beare
> Mr Spike Bludgeon
> Mr Mallory King
> Sir Joh. Nappleby
> Mr Jerry Pason
> M. Atlas Poireau
> Lord Simon Quinsey
> Miss Fan Sliver
> Mr Broderick Tourneur

Twenty minutes later the *Florabunda*, with one prolonged blast from her whistle and then three shorter ones, was under way.

CHAPTER 2

DETECTIVES

Sir Jon. Nappleby shifted his gaze. The fog sadly wanted individuality. Whereas the man who leaned against the rail some six feet astern, frowning gloomily over Nappleby's head into the monotonous brume which was all a sulky Atlantic afforded the eye, was distinctly out of the ordinary. Even, Nappleby thought (permitting himself a scrutiny discreetly veiled by vacuity of expression), fantastic. A *lusus naturae*.

The head, regrettably pyramidical, suggested some previous quasi-geological catastrophe in the course of which the brains had slidden sluggishly down into the jowls and the skull collapsed in order to prevent that vacuum so distasteful to Nature. A smaller pyramid was unimaginatively attached to the spot normally occupied by noses; the eyes and mouth were such triangular gashes as children make in Jack o' Lanterns. Just such a head, Nappleby thought, might some Cubist Frankenstein have manufactured from stray conic chunks of flesh, and poised it thus on an inverted pyramidal trunk. Or, the devotees of certain purveyors of 'science fiction' might have seen in this being the forerunner of an extraplanetary invasion: an ambassador from the inhabitants of Mars or of the moist and radiant Venus; the glass of fashion and the mould of form for a populace cuneiform, triquetrous, bald.

But, Nappleby reasoned more soberly, this was no Martian, but a fellow passenger. An American, by his clothing; a rich one, by — by what sign? One did not achieve greatness in Scotland Yard (where Nappleby was Assistant Commissioner) and retain any naïve and obsolete belief that mere transatlantic cadences, bulk, and assurance denote wealth. Yet something persuaded Nappleby that it was a millionaire who shared his vigil – but a millionaire not wholly at his ease: disturbed, indeed, by battering waves from the depth of some pyramidical despair.

Nappleby sighed. He had looked too long at his fellow voyager. The triangular man had observed his interest – was approaching. An acquaintanceship – in the very precincts of the foghorn, which even now let out a loud and tremolant wail – was about to be struck.

' – Paul Pry!'

'I beg your pardon?' Nappleby was uncertain. Admittedly his speculations had transgressed the complimentary; but surely their course had not been visible? An instant's reflection informed him, however, that the intonations had been those of inquiry rather than arraignment; and, in fact, the triangular lineaments were now being disposed in a pattern presumably intended to ingratiate.

The fog-blast vanished with an upward twist.

'Mr Paul Price?'

'Oh. No.' Nappleby shook his head.

'Oh.' His interlocutor appeared to have lost all interest.

'*My* name's Price.' A third man emerged from the fog which was now swathing even the promenade deck.

'Mr Price!' The pyramids swung about on their axis.

Nappleby considered the newcomer. Here, at least, one need not resort for similitude to realms of geometry or the pseudo-scientific. Here the most inveterate abstractionist must defer to the banal but insistent claim of the animal kingdom, and grant the deplorable resemblance of this Price to the common rat, *Rattus norvegicus* – or rather, one deduced from the voice and, again, the clothing – *americanus*.

'Mr Price!' The pyramidical millionaire had evidently no prejudice against the rodentine. Propitiation was becoming servility; the blubbery jowls quivered and flapped in frantic desire to oblige. 'I'm Anderson. Homer T. Anderson. I've been hoping to meet you on board, Mr Price – '

They walked away. The foghorn blew again, dispiritedly. Nappleby returned to contemplation of vaporous inanity. In this intrigue, if intrigue it were, he would not be involved. He would hope for a peaceful voyage, free from plots.

Nappleby sighed.

So few of his voyages had been *that*.

Jerry Pason said cheerfully: 'Well, it won't be long now, Stella. One more week, and we'll be back in the good old U.S.A.'

Stella Deet, Pason's attractive secretary, nodded. They stood looking into the fog from the promenade deck of the R.M.S. *Florabunda*.

'You certainly got a lot done in England, Chief,' she said. 'No one but you could have handled that case so well!'

'I *had* to do it well,' Pason said, 'when they sent to Los Angeles for me all the way from Peckham, England! But this trip home will be a holiday.'

'You need a rest, Chief,' Stella Deet said tenderly.

'Shucks,' the lawyer said, grinning. 'I don't know what a rest is, Stella, I – '

'I wonder who that officer is,' Stella Deet said as a man went past.

'The ship's Doctor,' Pason told her. 'He is a great poet.'

'Gosh, Chief,' said Stella Deet. She looked at him with wistful admiration. 'How can you tell these things just by looking?'

Pason smiled. 'Practice accounts for it in part,' he told her. 'And concentration. But this time I had help. I know from the kind and number of stripes on his sleeve that he is the Doctor, and my cabin steward told me the rest. I – ' He broke off.

'What is it?' Stella Deet asked quickly.

'Don't turn around,' Pason told her, tensely. 'But I'm curious about a man who's walking towards us. I have a feeling I've seen him before, or possibly seen his photograph.'

Stella Deet opened her handbag, whipped out a vanity case, and held it up to powder her nose. In the mirror she watched a small, ratlike man who was coming along the deck in their direction.

'I don't know, Chief,' she said in a quick low voice. 'But I think I've seen his picture somewhere.'

'Someone else is interested in him too,' the lawyer said.

A large man with a cone-shaped head hurried up behind

the small, ratlike man. He said, panting a little, 'Do you mind if I walk along with you again, Mr Price?'

The small, ratlike man shrugged. 'The deck's free,' he said. They disappeared from sight.

'Now I know who he is,' the lawyer said. 'He's Paul Price.'

'The columnist?' asked Stella Deet.

'Yes,' said the lawyer. 'I remember hearing he was on his way back to New York.'

'And do you know who the other man is?' Stella Deet asked.

'No,' Pason said. 'But he certainly seemed anxious to talk to Paul Price. I wonder – '

'Why,' Stella Deet asked, 'do you think there's anything fishy about it, Chief?'

'I don't know anything about it,' Pason told her. 'Just a hunch, that's all. Price has a bad reputation. I wouldn't be surprised if there should be some kind of trouble ahead.'

Miss Fan Sliver looked about her cabin contentedly. Surprisingly large, really, and *most* comfortable. At first, perhaps, it had seemed a trifle stark. But she had spread her travelling rug, with its cheery stripes, over the berth, and had hung on the walls small coloured prints of 'Bubbles', 'Cherry-Ripe', and 'The Black Brunswicker'. She could not, of course, hope to have many of her photographs about her on a sea voyage, but thirty or forty were placed here and there on the desk and on the little chest of drawers, where her Bible also reposed; and, all in all, the cabin now seemed almost homelike.

Miss Sliver, like her prints, was a little old-fashioned in appearance. Her mousy hair was fringed in the fashion set by Queen Alexandra. She wore a pink, grey, and orange merino dress, fastened at the throat by a large cameo brooch with the head of Minerva in intaglio. Over the dress she wore a black coatee. Her stockings were of wool.

Miss Sliver was deeply grateful to Providence for this opportunity to travel. An unexpected legacy took care of the passage, and a young American whose life she had once saved insisted, positively *insisted*, upon entertaining her in New York; so she need not be kept at home by the currency restrictions which made travel so very difficult for most

9

Britons. And now she could enjoy the voyage itself! One was certain to meet delightful people, from various backgrounds and with varied experiences; really it would be something to look back on for the rest of one's life.

Miss Sliver gathered up her knitting and opened her door. She hesitated for a moment with her hand still on the knob. A man stood with his back towards her. There was something furtive in his attitude. He was very evidently trying to see what was going on inside the next cabin.

Miss Sliver gave a dry little cough.

The man turned round sharply. Miss Sliver recognized him. The stewardess had pointed him out as a famous American gossip columnist, a Mr Price. He did not seem to mind Miss Sliver's having seen him, but brushed by her with a cold, indifferent stare from beady eyes.

Miss Sliver was not offended. Her appearance had too often stood her in good stead. Mr Price might have been startled to know just how many malefactors had been foiled by that dowdy, prim, insignificant air which had led him to disregard her.

An elderly woman came out of the cabin he had been peering into – a redoubtable woman with heavy iron-grey eyebrows and elaborately waved hair of a lighter grey. Miss Sliver felt a stir of curiosity. This passenger, also, was known to her by name. What interest could a gossipmonger have in the Honourable Mrs Chip-Ebberly?

Miss Sliver checked herself firmly. She was not engaged upon a case. As a private gentlewoman, she must not be inquisitive. Gripping her knitting-bag, she made her way carefully, noting the various turns and stairways (so *easy* to become lost!), towards the Lounge.

(*From the memoirs of Spike Bludgeon*)

The steward put his head in my door and asked, 'Did you ring, sir?'

'I've been ringing for the last five minutes,' I told him. I said it coldly, because I was pretty tired of waiting. Five minutes are a long wait when you want a drink the way I did.

'I'm sorry, sir. I didn't hear you before,' he said.

'If you're not sorry now, you're going to be,' I told him. I reached out and grabbed him by the arm. I dug my fingers in till I felt bone. His tray clattered to deck, and a surprised look came over his face. A little muscle in his cheek gave a twitch. You could tell he was yellow.

'Next time, come when I ring,' I told him. Still gripping him with one hand, I jammed the other into his gut just above the navel, nice and hard, and followed up with a slap across the face. You could hear two or three teeth crack.

His eyes shut. He sank down and slid through the doorway and across the passageway with the rolling of the ship.

I stepped out into the passage after him. Five or six fluffs were peeking out their cabin doors. They looked at me like I was God. I could tell what they wanted, but I wasn't in the mood.

A man's voice behind me said, 'Nice work!'

I whirled to face him. It was Paul Price.

'The service on this tub is too damned slow,' he said. 'Maybe that will help things a bit, speed them up. You must be Spike Bludgeon?'

'That's me, Mr Price,' I said.

'I'd like a little talk with you,' he said. 'Maybe we can work a trade. I've been thinking of running a story about you in my column. Spike Bludgeon – great detective, great lover.'

'Yeah?' I was pleased. My guts felt warm. A man likes recognition, and when it comes from a world-famous guy like Price . . .

'You've got a gun?'

I patted my armpit. 'Never without it. There she is. Quick and sure.'

'I may need protection. I've been finding out some things. My life may be in danger. Why, just a little while ago someone nearly gouged my eye out.'

Now he mentioned it, I could see his eye was red and inflamed. I was going to ask him about it when he gasped and put his hand to his mouth. He turned and dashed for the head. You could tell he was seasick.

Well, we could discuss things later. I kicked the steward out of the way, and headed for the bar.

'The Captain's table? Oh, rather,' said Lord Simon Quinsey with the prompt cheerfulness of one prepared to oblige in far more irksome matters than taking the seat assigned him.

Adjusting his monocle, Quinsey surveyed the Lounge as the Chief Steward glided away. A tall mirror, slightly yellowed, swaying with the regular motion of the ship, reflected his slim, elegant black and white, his sleek fair head, his general pose of vague, bland amiability.

'Oh, damn,' muttered his lordship. Mrs Chip-Ebberly, an old acquaintance of his sister-in-law the Duchess of Havers, had fixed him with a determined eye. He made his way dutifully towards her.

'I see we are to be table-mates, Lord Simon,' she began in the plangent tones which had opened innumerable bazaars. 'But in the most extraordinary company. One had never expected to dine with policemen. Indeed, I have no intention of doing so.'

Her intensity astonished Quinsey. 'Oh come,' he said affably. 'That won't do, Mrs C. The police are the coming thing, don't you know. Look at young Beauchamps. Look at Lord Lacey's boy. It's the new outlet for younger sons. The Church, the Bar, the Army, and the Yard.'

Mrs Chip-Ebberly gave him the pallid glare of the utterly humourless. 'One had forgotten that you engage in – *detection* yourself.'

'Oh, I used to dabble. But not for years – '

They turned at a rasping, aggressive voice from across the room. It proceeded from a man Quinsey had noticed earlier, a small grey man, singularly unprepossessing. Quinsey fancied that a native tendency to scuttle had been carefully corrected by an offensive and unconvincing swagger. 'Call this a *ship!*' this individual was saying. 'Seven days to cross the ocean! I ask you, is this the atomic age, or isn't it?'

Someone made an indistinguishable response. Clutching at the air as the *Florabunda* pitched, the small man repeated with even more strident truculence: 'Call it a ship? *I* call it a crappy old tub.'

Glancing at the varied indications of embarrassment, distaste, or amusement elicited by this pretty display of manners, Quinsey saw that one group had been affected rather more seriously. The officers in the Lounge looked with

superstitious horror at the Captain, who had just come in –
a tall man with a majestic carriage and a beard of the sort
attributed to Zeus in the better-known statues.

The passenger looked in the same direction and met the
Captain's eyes. He added deliberately: 'Nobody but a moron
would travel on a boat if he could get a plane reservation,
anyway.'

The Captain's green eyes dilated. Quinsey half expected to
see the blasphemer impaled on a trident; but the moment
passed: the Captain let out a long and regal snort, turned on
his heel, and left the room. In a graceful cascade of tinkles the
dinner-gong sounded. Quinsey found himself moving towards
the dining-saloon beside the First Officer.

'Who *is* that chap?' he asked.

'I don't know.' The First Officer repeated Quinsey's question to the Chief Steward.

'A Mr Price, sir.'

'Ah.'

'A pity', Quinsey suggested as in apology for the passengers
in general, 'to drive the Captain from his own table – '

'Oh, actually *that* doesn't matter,' said the First Officer
reassuringly. 'The Skipper never does eat down here anyway.
We just *call* it the Captain's table. If it hadn't been this
blighter Price, it would have been something else.'

'Why?' asked Quinsey, rather intrigued.

But the First Officer seemed to feel he had said too much.
'Oh – one thing or another,' he murmured. 'Shall we go in?'

Atlas Poireau sat at ease in the Lounge, twisted his large,
glossy black moustaches, and permitted his dinner to digest.

Only a few hours out, and already one sensed parties,
cliques, tensions! One could find food for thought in the
grotesque Mr Anderson, who was worried about something.
Or in the pretty, dark *jeune fille* who sat talking with the
fair, handsome Purser. Or in the American who had created
the scene just before dinner.

Poireau sighed. To the dispassionate observer of humanity,
the speed with which such a specimen as this journalist, *ce
monsieur* Paul Price, could engender wholehearted dislike,
among so many people who had never seen him before,

was of the highest interest. Instructive. And not without its amusing features.

But too often Poireau had seen such dislikes brew, in confined space, till they exploded into something more. Into hatred. Sometimes even . . .. murder.

'Mr Poireau?'

The ship's Doctor, a plump man with a pleasant face and round pale eyes, stood before him somewhat diffidently. At Poireau's invitation he took the next chair. He said eagerly: 'There's a great excitement at having so many detectives on board. It's an odd coincidence, isn't it?'

Poireau said, 'Coincidence, yes.'

'And the oddest thing is, none of you *look* like detectives! No one would know except from your names. And even when I heard them *I* didn't know – the First told me! I don't go in for that sort of thing. Of course, I would have known you were a *Frenchman*, Mr Poireau.'

Poireau said stiffly, 'I am a Belgian.'

The Doctor nodded as if this confirmed his statement. He went on, 'Now, as you're a detective, what would you make of *me*?'

Poireau looked at him coldly. It was *ennuyeux* to be informed that one's reputation was not known, and then to have one's abilities put to the test. He said a little coldly: '*Eh bien* . . . I should not have guessed, perhaps, without the aid of your stripes, that you were a medical man.'

The barb missed its effect. The Doctor said enthusiastically: 'I say, that's very impressive! Exactly. I am a doctor only because it gives me time for my *real* work. I am a poet!'

Poireau saw the journalist Price come up to the young, dark-haired girl and say something which made her turn scarlet. The Purser, who was still with her, jumped to his feet, clenched his fists. His eyes were blazing. The girl seized his arm. After a moment, he pulled himself away from her and strode from the room with an angry look at Price.

'Mr Poireau?'

With a start, Poireau returned his attention to the Doctor. 'A thousand pardons – '

'I said, Do you like poetry?'

Poireau said cautiously: 'Sometimes.'

'Well, I will read you a bit of my epic some day. When

14

would you care to hear it? It is called "Tipptoppus and Gazella". The first canto – ' He stopped, seeing that Poireau was again inattentive.

The little Belgian apologized again. 'But that child, she interests me,' he said.

'Oh. She's a Miss Price, I think. The niece of that chap who – '

'Ah, *oui*, I saw. It was offensive,' said Poireau. 'One does not insult the commander as he did.'

'Oh, but of course the Old Man's dotty anyway,' the Doctor said matter-of-factly. 'So you're interested in the lass, Mr Poireau? Is it as a detective, or as a Frenchman, eh?' He produced a leer which seemed odd on his round innocent face.

Poireau said calmly: 'You are mistaken, *mon cher docteur*. If Miss Price interests me, it is that she is the niece of her uncle. And also, a little, that she is very unhappy.'

Mallory King assured Paul Price for the twentieth time, wearily, that he didn't know why nine famous detectives happened to be aboard the *Florabunda*.

'Well, if you won't talk, I suppose you won't.' Price said raspingly.

Suddenly he turned green in the face, put his hand to his mouth, and dashed away.

With a thoroughly un-Christian satisfaction, Mallory watched him flee. Mallory was a kindly soul in normal circumstances, and a touch of seasickness is usually enough to make the whole world kin; but twenty minutes with Paul Price had led him to think that certain humanitarian laws might be suspended when one dealt with him.

Not *just* those twenty minutes of badgering and snooping, though. For many years Mallory, along with several million other Americans, had known Paul Price's name; and (since a detective must keep up with things) he had often run his eye over the cosy titbits of scandal Price peddled daily from coast to coast.

Yes, Mallory knew Paul Price.

Paul Price. Crest, *a keyhole and ear*. Motto: *Think no thing private*.

Moreover, King *père* was high up in the Manhattan police

force, and from him Mallory had heard things about Price that were not so widely known.

An unsavoury character, Price. Odoriferous. In fact, a stinkeroo.

Mallory turned. In the neighbouring group of passengers, conversation had turned on the tourist industry, Customs, and souvenirs.

'Speaking of souvenirs . . .' This was Homer T. Anderson, the pompous man with the turnip head. He had been drinking heavily and, with Price's hurried departure, he became suddenly self-assertive. 'Speaking of souvenirs, I'll show you all a little something I picked up. Wait here, all of you!' He stumbled over a chair as he hurried off.

Mallory looked at the group, mildly curious. A handful of officers – the First Officer, the Purser, the Doctor; a striking young blonde woman; Winifred Price; and – oddly – the Hon. Mrs Chip-Ebberly, a frosty dowagerial type. Mallory was puzzled at her remaining. But she was not merely present, but seemed unable to tear her eyes from Anderson as he returned dangling an object before them.

'Do you know what this is?' he demanded. 'It's a blackjack! A sap! You hear about those murders in London last month? Well, fellow I met in – in London,' said Mr Anderson thickly, 'fellow I met knew the cop that caught the killer, see? And he wangled this for me. For my collection. Swell little murder weapon, hey?' He passed it to the Doctor, who weighed it gravely in his hand.

'Aye, 'tis a cosh,' said the Doctor noncommittally. He held it out to its owner and, when the swaying and gesticulating Anderson paid no attention, tossed it on to a table.

'Well,' said Anderson, 'that's *my* souvenir of Merry England. None of your phony antiques for me. It's something for my collection.' He hiccoughed. ''Smy – 'smy *hobby*, murder weapons!'

'The fog's lifting,' somebody called from a porthole.

People drifted to look out. Muttering inaudibly, Anderson lurched from the room. Mallory wanted a closer look at the cosh, having a professional interest in such gadgets. He reached to pick it up.

The table was bare.

The table was bare, and the cosh was gone.

The cosh was gone!

Who could have taken it? Anderson had not picked it up
– Mallory could swear to that. But who else would want it?

Mallory grinned as he caught himself puzzling about so
elementary a matter. Analytical training should have told him
at once that at sea tables do not obey the laws of *terra firma*.
The blackjack, of course, had slipped to the deck with the
rolling of the ship. He bent over to pick it up.

Five minutes later, after a conscientious examination, he
straightened up.

The cosh was not on the deck either!

IT WAS GONE!

Broderick Tourneur took his drink and put three florins on
the tray. He watched the steward weave skilfully back to the
bar, avoiding the lurches of passengers who were not so sure
of foot.

Chief Detective-Inspector Broderick Tourneur was a very
tall man, with an air of extraordinary distinction. His face,
austerely chiselled, with dark brows that slanted upwards like
wings, insistently suggested at once the monk and the Spanish
grandee.

Looking about, he sighed inaudibly. First night out, and
already the passengers were dividing themselves into those
who hugged the bar till closing time and those who retired
with novels; those who entertained and those who bored;
those who lionized and those who were lions – 'and of the
latter,' Tourneur acknowledged with a grimace, 'I am apparently one.'

He found it hard to classify two women passengers who
sat near him. They were not together. One was slight, pretty,
and rather touchingly young. In spite of a sophisticated black
frock, *décolleté* and outrageously expensive, the main
impression she conveyed was of being a 'nice' American
college girl; her dark hair, cut modishly short, was as fluffy
and soft as a kitten's. Tourneur fancied he had seen her earlier
talking with the Purser. Now she sat alone, sipping slowly at
a lemonade, and rebuffed with an almost *farouche* directness
the occasional tentative overtures of other passengers.

The other woman was at least ten years older. She was a
blonde with blue eyes, a full scarlet mouth, and a dazzling

complexion. She looked self-conscious and yet vacant. What roused Tourneur's interest was the fact that she, too, seemed determined to be left alone. But not because *you're* shy, my girl, Tourneur guessed. I wonder whom you're waiting for? A moment later he ejaculated inwardly: Good Lord! Can that really be the answer?

Advancing towards her with the doubly repulsive manner of the unalluring male who conquers by other than personal charms and the poor sailor who is uncertain of the state of his stomach, came the columnist Paul Price. The blonde directed a brilliant smile at him. But he interrupted his progress to speak to the dark girl, who sat gloomily regarding the carpet.

'For Christ's sake, Winifred,' said Mr Price elegantly. 'What are you doing here? I can't keep my eye on you every minute. You ought to be in bed. You go to your stateroom right now.'

Winifred Price looked up with a start that sent her handbag hurtling to the floor. Her eyes flashed. For an instant, Tourneur thought she might resist this courteous exhortation; but Price had already gone by, and after a moment she rose slowly. Tourneur, whose manners were always extremely good, picked up her bag and held it out to her, bowing slightly. She muttered, 'Thank you.' As their eyes met, he was appalled to see two tears roll down her cheeks.

'Well, little Dolores, so you were lonesome?' Mr Price murmured to the blonde in a thick and fulsome undertone. His button eyes gleamed, and he totally ignored the proximity of Tourneur.

He is like a rodent, Tourneur thought. And an amorous rodent at that.

Price managed, in lighting her cigarette, to fondle little Dolores' hand, and she responded with a carefully calculated languishing heave of her bosom.

Oh Lord, Tourneur thought. How beastly. How unutterably, foully beastly. Fastidiously he averted his glance. He finished his drink at a gulp, and left the room.

(Trajan Beare – from the notebook of Ernie Woodbin)

We'd been in London three weeks, but I still did a double-take every time I realized that Beare, who was so jittery about

New York traffic that he only left his house on Thirty-sixth Street once or twice a year, had actually travelled three thousand miles, and not even on solid ground. Even when I remembered how high up the highup in Washington was who'd persuaded him to make the trip, I couldn't believe it. But I can't say any more about that – security reasons.

There were two ways of handling the agony, air or sea, and going he'd chosen to get it over quick. Then we'd had to come down at Gander three times with engine trouble, and then hit every air pocket between there and Shannon, so once I'd got him settled in a hotel in London I expected he'd stay there the rest of his life. But either I'd underestimated his patriotism or he couldn't stand the food. He wanted to come home. He chose the sea this time, only he insisted on getting the trip over with right away, even if it meant passage on a slower ship than the *United States*. This meant I couldn't squeeze in the week I'd wanted in Paris.

Normally this would have made a coolness between us, and when I went into Beare's cabin and saw him sitting up in bed with a few acres of yellow pyjama wrapped around his four hundred pounds, and his life-jacket within easy reach, I thought of a number of possible cracks, such as saying the Captain was alarmed about a list to starboard, starboard being the side Beare's cabin was on; but I refrained. For one thing it wasn't up to my usual level and also I admit I just didn't have the heart. So I merely asked, Did he realize that if we'd flown we'd be a third of the way home by now?

'Of course, for myself I *like* an ocean voyage,' I said enthusiastically. 'Now, if you get up early tomorrow and join in the fun, you'll wish you had two weeks instead of only one!'

Beare closed his eyes. 'It is understood that I remain here until we dock. I do not intend to leave this room.'

'You'd meet some interesting people. One of them I've often heard you mention – Paul Price.'

Beare opened his eyes and repeated, 'Paul Price?' He would have used the same tone if I'd informed him that bubonic plague had broken out on B-deck.

'Yeah. The great man. You'll be glad to know that your opinion of him is shared by everyone on board, including me. Maybe you'll see him anyway – he wants to talk with you. Write you up in his column.'

'Ernie.'

'Sir?'

'It is understood that no one is to enter this stateroom without my permission. Should Mr Price attempt to interview me you will prevent him. Forcibly, if necessary.'

'Okay. But I warn you he may try. He thinks it's a funny coincidence there should be nine detectives aboard. So do I.'

'Nine detectives?'

'Yes, sir. Mallory King is here, and Jerry Pason. You know about them. Pason has his secretary with him – Will it be all right if I start calling you "Chief"? Then there's Spike Bludgeon, you'd love to meet him; and Sir Jon. Nappleby and Broderick Tourneur and Atlas Poireau and Lord Simon Quinsey. Also a Limey lady detective, Miss Sliver; she's at my table, but she's over my age limit. Come to think of it,' I said earnestly, 'she wouldn't be bad for you. You'd have your profession in common, and she could knit your socks. She's great at conversation, she asks educational questions about orchid-growing and the American system of government.'

Beare had closed his eyes again, but I guessed he wasn't asleep; so I went on: 'Then there are the ones I'd like to marry – passengers, I mean, not detectives. One of them is named Winifred, but I've decided not to take her because I don't want to call Price Uncle Paul; and anyway she's interested in the Purser. Now if only I had a uniform I could compete – '

'Ernie.' Beare opened his eyes. 'No more coyness. I appeal to your magnanimity. Revenge later, if you will. Not here, not now.'

'Yes, sir. The other one is Dolores Despana, an actress. So far I don't know any reason for not choosing her. That's all I have to report, except the officers. The Captain is said to be a loony. The Doctor writes poetry. Maybe you'd like him to drop in, he loves to read it aloud to people. The First Mate needs a haircut. The Purser's all right, except for being my rival with Winnie – '

Beare kept his eyes shut, and said, 'Good night.' I guessed he meant it, so I headed out and off to my own berth.

CHAPTER 3

MURDER

The *Florabunda* ploughed on through grey seas and pearly fog at a dogged fifteen knots. The Captain signed the records of her progress: he signed, he sighed, he stroked his long beard yearningly. When not on watch, the First Officer kept a vigilant eye on his commander, talked with his friend the ship's Doctor, or read. The Purser laboured over invoices and Customs forms, and the Doctor (with reluctant digressions to dole out pills or attend to cuts and bruises) over his epic, 'Tipptoppus and Gazella'. The other officers and the crew pursued their duties according to an immemorial routine.

But the crossing was no routine matter for the passengers. The presence of nine detectives could not fail to be sensational. In vain did the detectives themselves protest (quite truthfully) that only chance had put them all on the same ship at the same time. Who could be expected to believe that if Lord Simon Quinsey visited Mr Trajan Beare it was simply to discuss food, a topic of passionate concern to them both; that if he took tea with Miss Fan Sliver it was to share with her his newborn enthusiasm for the verse of Tennyson? Nine famous detectives were too many to take calmly. And some wit declared that, under the circumstances, if a murder did not exist one would have to be invented.

Nevertheless, while life in general imitates art, in any given case the ideal schemes of the imagination are not usually viable. And so, with a single exception, everyone aboard the *Florabunda* was startled to hear, just after the second breakfast of the trip, that the gossip columnist Paul Price had been found dead — murdered — his head bashed in.

A deck steward discovered the body, amidships on the

21

starboard side of the main deck. The tarpaulin with which he had covered a pile of folding chairs last night was disarranged; when he moved it he saw a man's body wedged in between the chairs and the angle of the bulkhead so tightly that it had not been dislodged by the rolling of the ship. The steward recognized the face. He ran to notify the head deck steward, who notified the Chief Steward, who caught the First Officer's eye at the very moment when the Captain was approaching in the course of his daily tour of inspection, with an attendant train of officers.

The First Officer fell back to listen to the Chief Steward. 'What's that?' he exclaimed. 'What, what?'

The Captain looked back with an inquiring frown.

'A murder, sir,' Mr Waggish told him. 'One of the passengers. Mr Price has been murdered.'

'Good,' said the Captain simply. He resumed his progress along the deck.

'But – have you any orders, sir?'

The Captain swung about and blinked at him.

'That is – if the man was killed, sir,' Mr Waggish suggested diffidently, 'shouldn't we take steps to find out who did it?'

'Who *did* it?' the Captain repeated. His eyes glittered with a sudden green flame. It died; he replied indifferently. 'Very well, Mr Waggish. The matter is in your hands.' He moved grandly on.

The First Officer stared after him with a baffled expression. He became suddenly aware that their conversation had been eagerly followed by a large number of passengers, as many as could squeeze within earshot.

'Look here,' said the Purser in a low voice, his pink face kindling. 'We've got those detectives on board, haven't we?'

Mr Waggish looked at him gratefully. 'So we have,' he said in relief. 'That's no' such a bad idea, Tom.' He looked about at the passengers, and turned to the Purser again. 'Send someone to them,' he said. 'Ask if they'll have the goodness to meet me at – er – at the scene of the crime, and confer about this business.'

'Someone has murdered Mr Price,' the First Officer explained, 'if it wasn't accident, that is, or suicide, but I don't see how it could be, the way the body's crammed into the corner.

Well, we've never had this happen before, and I don't quite know how to tackle it, and I thought – I speak for the commander of this vessel when I say – that is, I'd be damn' grateful if all hands would give me their expert assistance and advice and – er – assistance.'

He looked at the detectives hopefully, anxiously out of bright blue eyes, as their heads rose and fell rhythmically against a back-drop of swirling fog.

The request was not completely successful. Ernie Woodbin explained that his employer, Mr Beare, never worked except for a fee even on dry land. Spike Bludgeon was in bed, seasick. Miss Sliver demurred out of modesty: her services could not be necessary with so many *distinguished* investigators at hand. Simon Quinsey declined, too. For an instant his nostrils quivered like those of an old warhorse scenting battle; but he shook his head. 'No, no,' he said austerely, 'I gave up all that sort of thing years ago,' and went below to read *Idylls of the King*.

The others were touched to acquiescence by the blend of formality, bashfulness, and nautical unwordliness in Mr Waggish's appeal.

'But the mechanics are awkward,' Sir Jon. Nappleby frowned. 'We cannot investigate *en masse*. Yet we are bound to overlap unless we share such information as we glean.'

'We can keep in touch through Mr Waggish,' suggested Mallory King. 'He can act as a sort of clearing-house.'

'Certainly, whatever you gentlemen say,' said that officer cautiously. 'Only, you see, I've no experience in this line – '

'So much the better,' smiled Broderick Tourneur. 'A Watson is needed, and you may play the part. You shall be Watson, sir, to the lot of us.'

The Doctor arrived and stooped over Price's body to examine it as well as its cramped position permitted. When he straightened up everyone looked at him expectantly.

'The paths of glory', the Doctor told them, 'lead but to the grave.' He supplied this information with a conclusiveness which suggested that he considered it adequate to any just demands which might be made of him. But presently, as an afterthought, he explained that death was due to a blow on the head inflicted by (in this area of diction at least the Doctor was not sensitive to cliché) a 'blunt instrument'.

'*When* was he killed?' Mr Waggish asked him.

'I can't tell here.' The Doctor sounded cross. 'Have him taken below.'

When the body was moved, the detectives saw something which had been concealed hitherto: a woollen scarf, with bright red and yellow stripes, quite sodden with salt water which had flowed back and forth across it with the tilting of the deck. Lifting it carefully, Sir Jon. Nappleby disentangled a smallish object which had been caught up in one end of it – a black briar pipe.

'A new one,' he observed.

'It has never been used,' Jerry Pason agreed. He explained: 'I can tell because there are no teeth-marks on the stem and no traces on the bowl of smoke or of tobacco ash.'

'We have them on sale in the ship's store,' said the Purser. 'I don't suppose it's heavy enough for the weapon?'

The First Officer said suddenly: 'The weapon – a *blunt instrument?* Why, one of the passengers has a cosh. He was showing it in the Lounge.'

Mallory King nodded. 'But it was stolen!' He related how Homer T. Anderson's blackjack had disappeared.

There was no trace of it, or of any other blunt instrument at all, on deck.

'Do you think it could have been thrown overboard?' the First Officer asked. He flushed a little and added apologetically. 'I mean, it seems *possible* . . . I'm only a lubber when it comes to detecting.'

'It's an intelligent guess,' said Chief Inspector Tourneur kindly. 'The deck is open here. But the *great* question of course, is – ' He paused significantly, and the other detectives nodded.

'Aye?' Mr Waggish ventured after a respectful pause.

They were silent. Then: 'If you think for a moment,' said Atlas Poireau, 'you will see for yourself what it is, Mr Waggish.'

The apprenticeship of Watson had begun.

Price's body was carried into the little consulting-room which adjoined the Doctor's cabin on B-deeck. Into the cabin crowded the detectives with the First Officer and the Purser, who seemed unable to tear himself away from the investigation, though he was long overdue at his office. They found seats amid a litter of pipe-tobacco, beer-tins, oranges, neckties, and countless loose sheets of lined foolscap paper which were written over in a slashing hand in bold black ink, and slithered back and forth over table, deck, bunk, and settee with the rolling and pitching of the ship.

The contents of Paul Price's pockets now lay in a green box on the doctor's desk, with the scarf and the pipe which had been under his body. Mr Waggish, handling them gingerly, as if they might explode, passed them about for inspection.

The passport recorded that Price had been born in Duluth, Minnesota, in 1906, was a journalist, and had travelled in France and the United Kingdom.

'Then his wallet.' The First Officer opened a brown alligator case. 'An identification card; a driver's licence, U.S.A.; a pound note; and ... seventy-five, seventy-six dollars in American bills.'

The door to the consulting-room opened, and the Doctor burst in, in his shirt-sleeves. He made his way to the untidy bookshelf over his desk and, one hand outstretched to steady himself against the *Florabunda's* tossing, began to search for a book. He shoved aside *Jerusalem Delivered*, an odd volume of Browning's *Poems*, and a battered Rhyming Dictionary, and came at last to a huge book in half-calf, which he spread out on the desk. It was a medical encyclopaedia. The Doctor flipped through the pages, read a paragraph or two with furious concentration, banged it shut, and darted back into the other room.

Mr Waggish cleared his throat. 'Here is a packet of Players. It's pretty well crumpled. There are only fourteen – fifteen fags left. And here's another packet of twenty, still sealed. And a handkerchief, a key-ring, and a book of American Express traveller's cheques.'

The door flew open again; the Doctor lunged again at his encyclopaedia. Thumbing the pages, he found his place once more, and reread the page.

Mr Waggish coughed. There was silence till the door had closed again behind the Doctor. Then he said, 'There's nothing else but some odd coins.'

'*What are they?*' inquired Atlas Poireau.

The First Officer obediently sorted them out and counted them. 'Three French pieces, and a torn hundred-franc note rolled up with the coins. Then there's . . . Ah, four half-crowns, two florins, two shillings, two sixpences, and a half-penny. And a fifty-cent piece, four quarters, and three dimes.'

Tourneur asked: 'Did he leave any valuables with you, Purser?'

'Nothing at all. His – Miss Price left her cheques and her passport with us for safe-keeping, but *he* did not.'

'His niece! That reminds me,' said the First Officer compunctiously. 'We ought to notify her. I never thought to.'

'I happened to see Miss Price,' said the Purser, 'and spoke to her. She had already heard. She – she is very much upset.'

The Doctor came in, pulling on his coat. 'Well,' he announced briskly. 'It's a nasty wound. A single blow did it, too. Very efficient.'

'When did it happen?' several voices asked.

'Ah, well, there are many factors to be taken into consideration,' said the Doctor, with an involuntary glance towards his encyclopaedia. 'The temperature, don't you know, and the – '

'Well, but roughly?' the First Officer cut in unceremoniously.

'Between eleven last night and two this morning.'

'You'll do a post-mortem, of course,' Mallory King said blandly.

'Oh, if you like,' said the Doctor without enthusiasm. His eye fell on one of the loose sheets of his manuscript, and without transition, with a sudden access of zest, he read aloud:

' "What though", Tipptoppus cried, "my men be slain in this fierce strife?
What though", he somewhat loudly cried, "I risk my own dear life?
To see the Gods come down to earth and mortal men accost,
To see their spears hurled fore and aft, their faerie lances tossed,
I rate my life a gudgeon's worth, and count the World Well Lost!" '

26

Frowning, he abstracted a pen from the litter on his desk, and began to make corrections in his verse.

Mr Waggish looked at the detectives hesitantly. 'I suppose it's still too early to give us any notion who the killer is?'

At the expression on their faces he turned slowly red. He was abashed to the point of speechlessness.

'But, monsieur,' said Atlas Poireau at last, not ungently, 'it is not the affair of a *moment*, do you not see, to find a murderer! *Not even for us!* But rest assured, Mr Waggish, we will find him; we will find him, we will rout him out, though it be the Captain of the *Florabunda* himself!'

PART TWO

CHAPTER 4

ATLAS POIREAU

Atlas Poireau cast an approving glance about the Lounge – at its square carpets, its careful, regular arrangement of chairs and sofas and tables.

What Poireau liked about an ocean trip was not the ocean, that great waste of space and energy, nor the superabundance of fresh air, nor (*bon Dieu!*) the ceaseless swaying and tossing. What he liked was the tidiness of the vessel itself. Everything balanced, port and starboard. Economy. Precision. Names and numbers and labels. Ropes coiled neatly, gleaming brass, daily scrubbings and hosings. An efficient hierarchy, discipline, order. Everything, in fact, shipshape. He rolled the word on his tongue. *Shipshape.*

And then – murder!

The reason why Poireau had consented to aid in this investigation was his outrage at the breach of order the murder represented. It meant an end of quiet; a *brouhaha*; a deluge of questions, exclamations, gossip – and, no doubt, of lies.

And it exposed regrettable human weaknesses in that so admirable hierarchy. Poireau groaned inwardly as he recalled the deplorable unconcern of the Captain – the First Officer's hesitancy – the Doctor's – the Doctor's . . . Fervently Poireau prayed that he might not be stricken down with any serious disease whilst on board the R.M.S. *Florabunda*.

So far, a couple of hours after the discovery of Price's body, investigation had yielded little. It was known that Price had dined as usual. Much later, about eleven-twenty, the bar steward remembered serving him. Several people had noticed him talking with Mr Homer T. Anderson on deck, not far from where his body had been found this morning, but no one could say *exactly when* this had been. With the irresponsibility which overtakes most landsmen at sea, they had paid no attention to the hour. They could only say it was before midnight, by which time practically everyone had turned in.

A high voice asserted: 'It's the work of a *gang*, you see. This Paul Price was the leader. They called him "the Rat".'

Poireau raised his eyebrows and looked towards the voice. In a corner of the Lounge, three elderly women were talking. Moving closer, he listened unashamedly.

A second woman said: 'And the stewardess told me quite confidentially, that that is why all these detectives are aboard! But it was not the gang that killed Mr Price, my dear. His niece . . .' The rest was a whisper.

The Hon. Mrs Chip-Ebberly nodded. She said: 'I saw her with my own eyes coming in from deck. She was the very picture of guilt. Her face was scarlet. I was shocked – '

Mrs Chip-Ebberly noticed Poireau. She frowned. Poireau bowed affably. With a sweeping glance that took in all the marks of the foreigner, from his polished patent-leather shoes to his glossy black moustache, she sniffed. She made a faint inclination of her head.

Poireau was puzzled. Gossip, that was to be expected. But not of Mrs Chip-Ebberly. In her it seemed – disorderly. It was out of character.

Poireau knew the Ebberly tradition. He had stayed once at the family place – charged with recovering some stolen jewels. There had been the family peacocks on the terrace, the family ghost, the family Rubens, marked 'Doubtful' in the catalogues, the quite undoubted family diamonds, the family library, the . . . But that, of course, was before the war. Now, one never knew. Things had changed.

Still, one did not expect a Mrs Chip-Ebberly to change in deference to a mere war! What had shaken her so that she chattered loosely with other old ladies?

Thoughtfully, Poireau made his way to the cabin which the First Officer had set up as a headquarters for the investigation.

With Mr Waggish were Winifred Price and Homer T. Anderson.

Winifred Price sat very upright. Her eyes were red, her face pale; she held a crumpled damp handkerchief tightly in her right hand. In her tweed skirt and white blouse, with her dark hair rumpled, she looked childlike and defenceless.

The First Officer turned a harassed face towards the little Belgian. He exclaimed: 'Mr Poireau! Good! Maybe you can help.'

Anderson stared at Poireau out of cold, pale, triangular eyes. Poireau returned his gaze with urbanely concealed dislike. A geometric, regular, symmetrical face – yes. But it did not please. It was not – *sympathique*. Instinctively, Poireau patted the top of his own smooth, egg-shaped head.

'You come to tell us that you were with Mr Price last night?' he inquired innocently.

Anderson almost shouted: 'So you've heard about that, too! I don't deny I saw him. But I wasn't the *last* one to see him. *She* was. You'll find she killed him!'

He pointed at Winifred Price, who looked defiantly at him without saying a word.

'Ah! You saw Mademoiselle attack her uncle? That does, indeed, forward our investigation,' Poireau said smoothly.

'Saw – Of course I didn't *see* her kill him! But I saw them talking. She was with him on deck after I was.'

Poireau said: 'And you hasten to let the authorities know! I felicitate you on your public spirit.'

The First Officer said indignantly: 'I call it a bloody rotten thing to do!' He added quickly: 'I beg your pardon, Miss Price.'

Anderson said almost uncomfortably: 'It's plain self-defence. People have been saying that *I* was the last one to see Price.'

'You can supply a *motive* for Mademoiselle, also, no doubt?'

Anderson regained momentum. He said: 'Price was rich! She's his heir. She hated him; he told me himself she was giving him a lot of trouble.'

'You knew Mr Price well, one gathers.'

'Hardly knew him. We just had a word now and then.'

'You were perhaps interested in his – work?'

Anderson's face purpled. He demanded: 'Why should I be?'

'I do not know,' Poireau confessed. 'You are not yourself, I imagine, a journalist?'

'I'm a businessman. But never mind about me –'

'Ah! And may one ask, what business?'

Anderson glared. 'Business,' he said.

'Ah – *merci*,' Poireau said dryly. 'But last evening, monsieur, you discussed with this Mr Price, whom you scarcely know, his intimate family affairs – his relations with his niece?'

Anderson said: 'That was just in passing. We were having a friendly talk and a smoke, just before I went to bed.'

'And *how*', Poireau asked, 'do you suggest that Miss Price killed her uncle?'

'Why – they say he was hit on the head.'

'With what?'

Anderson seemed to pull himself in. He asked cautiously: 'You mean they don't know what the weapon was?'

Poireau said: 'Not yet.'

'Then –' Anderson's pale eyes went towards the porthole. It was as clear as if he had said, *Then it will never be found*. An odd look passed over his grotesquely moulded face.

He is relieved, thought Atlas Poireau.

Anderson stood up. He said belligerently: 'I'm leaving. I've told you all I can.'

Poireau made no effort to detain him. But he removed the cover from the green box which had been brought here from the Doctor's cabin.

'Monsieur Anderson! You forget something.' He held out the red and yellow muffler which had been found under Price's body.

Anderson looked blankly at it. 'What, that scarf? It isn't mine. Never saw it before.'

He went out.

The First Officer asked: 'Don't you think the muffler belonged to Mr Price?'

'I think it unsafe to take anything for granted. But we can ascertain. Mademoiselle, can you tell us if this was your uncle's?'

Winifred Price looked at the muffler dully. 'I don't know – Why, yes, I do know!' she said more energetically. 'It can't be his. He bought one in London because he didn't have any,

34

he said; and the one he bought was the Royal Stuart tartan. But what does that have to do with who killed him?'

'Nothing, perhaps. One merely inquires. But, mademoiselle, you have not had much opportunity to speak, and yet you have probably something to say.'

'Only that it isn't true!' said the girl. 'I did see Uncle Paul, near the place where he was – killed. But I didn't do it! And it was quite early when I left him, well before half past eleven; it was closer to quarter past.'

'And after that, mademoiselle?'

'I went to bed,' said Winifred Price. She looked directly at him, and her fingers closed hard on her handkerchief.

The First Officer glanced at his watch and said worriedly, 'I'm due on the bridge – '

Poireau rose and held the door open. 'Mademoiselle, will you permit me to talk with you again, say in fifteen minutes?'

She said dispiritedly, 'I'll be in my cabin.'

As the door closed Mr Waggish said heatedly: 'Imagine anyone accusing a nice kid like that of murder! Poor lass. What a bastard!'

'He is ungentlemanly, yes,' Poireau agreed, correctly disentangling the First Officer's meaning. It was not the first occasion he had to marvel at the chivalrous propensities of the English. And sailors, he knew, are a particularly sentimental lot.

'But you'll clear her, won't you?' Mr Waggish continued, his blue eyes appealing to Poireau from his tanned face.

'If she is innocent, *certainement*. We must first ascertain the truth.'

The First Officer said, with an unexpected turn for generalization, 'That is not always, easy, though.'

Poireau smiled. He said: 'For some, *non!* But *Atlas Poireau never fails!*'

Mr Waggish was impressed. He said eagerly: 'I'm glad that you're investigating, Mr Poireau. Everything seems very confused to me. And I wish you would tell me one thing before I have to go. What is the *great question?* You chaps said on deck that there's one "great question". But I don't see – '

'Ah, *oui*. It is a question indeed. Only consider, my friend.' Poireau paused dramatically. 'You have decided to kill a man.

35

You find him alone on deck. You strike him down. He falls – he is dead. It is dark. No one has seen. Very well. Now what, I ask you? Do you push and pull and shove this man across the deck and into a tiny cramped space and then drag a heavy canvas over him?' Poireau paused again. '*Or do you simply push him over the rail?* Why, with all of the Atlantic Ocean to abet you, do you deliberately leave the evidence of your crime behind?' Mr Waggish was chagrined. 'I see! Now that you point it out – why, no one but an imbecile would have left the body on board!'

Poireau shook his head in reproof. 'You are too hasty, *mon cher*. I can, offhand, think of three simple reasons. First: the murderer is not strong enough to raise the body to the necessary height. Though Mr Price was, remember, a small man.'

'But that would mean a woman.'

'*Peut-être*. Second: the criminal *wants* the body to be found! He wants to avoid a verdict of "Presumed death" merely. He wishes, maybe, to avoid delay in the probate of a will.'

'But – And the third reason?'

Poireau said: 'Ah, *mon ami* – think for yourself!'

Poireau knocked three firm knocks, regularly timed, on the precise centre of the door.

Winifred Price called immediately: 'Come in!'

She had taken advantage of the past quarter-hour to freshen herself. Her hair was smooth, her face no longer shiny. But she was so pale that her lipstick stood out in a garish streak.

Poireau took the seat she offered him. He said: 'Mademoiselle, I omitted just now to offer my condolences. You must forgive me.'

She asked bitterly: 'Do people offer sympathy to – to murderers?'

He said gently: 'My child, you are, I think, melodramatic.'

'You don't think I killed my uncle?'

'*Did* you, mademoiselle?'

'No!' said Winifred Price. 'No, I didn't. Honestly! I don't know why that Mr Anderson says I did. You'd think he had a grudge against me, but I never even saw him before this trip. And the other passengers – they look at me as if – as if . . . It was bad enough before. They acted as if I was *poison*, just because – '

She bit her lip and stared hard at the porthole, over Poireau's head.

Poireau said invitingly: 'Tell me, mademoiselle. I do not mean about last night, simply. Tell me about your uncle and yourself.'

Something in his face seemed to encourage the girl. She began in a halting way: 'It's hard to explain. He was my guardian, but I never really knew him. I was always at boarding-school, or camp, and then college. But he paid for everything. I just took it for granted when I was a kid. I never really thought about him.

'And then at college I began to realize. The girls would say something about "Paul Pry's latest" (that's what people call him, you know), and then they'd remember I was there and be embarrassed. And then there was the time he was sued for libel and it was all over the front pages. And one day in class my sociology professor talked about him and said he was a symptom of the decay of American culture. He didn't know Paul Price's niece was at the lecture, of course. But I thought I'd die.'

'Not easy, *non*,' Poireau murmured gravely.

'But the bad part was, I couldn't stand up for him! What people said was true. Of course, it was very *understandable*. He was suffering from a deep feeling of inferiority which he never acknowledged overtly. He overcompensated for it by aggressiveness. Sadistic and – and erotic aggressiveness!'

She looked darkly at Poireau, who gave a respectful nod. She went on less glibly: 'He was a lot *worse* than outsiders knew. He would . . . ! Well, for instance, once when I was going to visit my room-mate, he told me to find out all I could about her family. He wanted something he could use for scandal; her father was going to run for Congress. I said I wouldn't be a spy, and we had an awful fight.'

She looked at Poireau and bit her lip again. 'And, you see, all the time I had to be *grateful* to him. I owed everything to him. And I didn't cut loose, I was a minor, and besides I'm a moral coward.'

She added gloomily: 'Now I'll go through the rest of my life with a guilt complex. In ten years, I'll be neurotic.'

Poireau gazed at her. 'In your college, mademoiselle, you doubtless studied many subjects – you studied psychology perhaps?'

'I took two courses in it! Why?'

Poireau bowed his head. 'I wondered, merely . . . But, *enfin*, you did go abroad, *n'est-ce pas*? You escaped?'

'They let me take my Junior year abroad. I took courses at the Sorbonne. It was wonderful! No one knew about my uncle. I met someone and got engaged. He's American and he knows about Paul Price, but he doesn't blame *me*. So – well, I wrote to my uncle and said I was going to marry Llewelyn; that's his name, Llewelyn. There was no answer, but the next thing I knew Uncle Paul was in Paris. He had a ghastly fight with Llewelyn, accusing him of being a fortune-hunter. And he made me come home with him. We went to London first, and we were going to fly home, but something happened.'

'*What* happened, mademoiselle?'

Winifred Price shook her head. 'He didn't really explain. He came into the hotel looking terribly pleased with himself and said maybe Llewelyn had done him a *service* by bringing him over, because he'd come across two nice pieces of business.'

'Ah!' Poireau leaned forward eagerly. 'Did he explain?'

'He must have meant he'd found material for the column. I remember he said something about tittle-tattle. "Someone has tattled," I guess he said. And then he told me we would be sailing on the *Florabunda*. That's all. Only it's been awful on board ship too, because he thinks – he thought everyone who was human to me was after his money.'

Poireau murmured: 'I seem to recall an incident in the Lounge. The young officer – '

Winifred turned red. 'Yes. That was typical, Monsieur Poireau. We were just talking, and my uncle came and told Tom – the Purser – that he would report him for misbehaviour with a passenger! It was horrible. I hated him!' She caught her tongue and looked at Poireau aghast. 'But last night it wasn't like that, honestly! I don't mean I'd forgiven him, but we didn't quarrel.'

'What *did* happen last night?'

'Nothing! I was on deck, I saw him, and spoke to him for a minute or two. That was all.'

Poireau's sense of order was offended. He said severely: 'Surely not *all*, mademoiselle. No detail can be ignored.'

'All right. Well – I wanted to show him I wasn't *immature*. I asked him for a cigarette, very calmly and politely.'

'And he, mademoiselle – was he also calm and polite? Did he give you a cigarette?'

'Well, no – he happened to be out of them; but he wasn't so rude as he'd been before. He was quite pleased about something. He said the ocean wasn't a bad place for a deal.'

'And that was all?'

'Yes. Except that I asked him if he could exchange some money for me.'

Poireau felt a tingling sensation. He asked quietly: 'Why, mademoiselle?'

'Why? I had more English money left than I could use up before landing, that's all, and he'd mentioned being down to his last halfpenny; so he was glad to take some of my money for his dollars – '

'How much, mademoiselle?'

'Oh, five or six dollars; it wasn't much – '

'*How much did you give him, mademoiselle?*'

She passed a hand wearily across her forhead. 'Does it matter?' But at Poireau's pained expression she answered hastily: 'I gave him two pound notes.'

Poireau was silent for a moment. Then he asked: 'And after that?'

'I went in, and I – went to bed.'

Her head went back as if she were bracing herself against another question, but Poireau only got to his feet and told her mildly:

'*Merci, mademoiselle.*'

He found Mr Homer T. Anderson on deck.

Anderson said: 'Look, I don't like all this snooping! Bad enough having a murder. Now all this snooping about the ship, snooping into people's private affairs! I didn't pay good passage money to have the police going into my private affairs.'

Poireau repeated thoughtfully: '*Passage* . . . Do you know, monsieur, I have wondered about that.'

'Huh?'

Poireau explained: 'The *Florabunda* is not the most rapid of ships. Nor is any ship so swift as a plane. To find a man of affairs like yourself, a businessman, a financier, aboard, is – of interest! One would expect, rather, to find you on the aeroplane. *Zip* – New York to Le Bourget! *Zip* – London to New York!'

He cocked his head and regarded Anderson inquiringly.

Anderson seemed baffled by his volatility. He replied stiffly: 'I couldn't get plane reservations. Weather conditions.'

'Ah! Like Monsieur Price.'

'What the devil do you mean?'

Poireau raised his eyebrows. 'But did you not know?' he lied smoothly. 'He too was aboard this ship because of difficulty with plane reservations. I thought you might have discussed it with him. It is the sort of topic discussed on shipboard, *n'est-ce pas*, by persons who are not intimate, but who are amicable . . . Your relations with Monsieur Price were amicable?'

Anderson's distrustfulness reached a new peak. He grunted: 'Huh? Were what?'

Poireau said humbly: 'Perhaps I misuse a word. I am not, you understand, English or American, and have not your command of the language! I meant to ask if you were on good terms with him.'

'Sure we were! We stood right there last night,' said Anderson, pointing to a part of the railing to which their walk along the deck had brought them, 'and we talked. We just talked in a very friendly way about the weather and the food. Nothing in particular.'

'And it was here, perhaps, that you offered him the cigarette?'

'That's right. Or, as a matter of fact, *he* offered *me* one. We were friendly, see? His cigarettes were Players, and I hate them, but I took one – to be polite.'

Poireau drew a deep breath. He said ambiguously: 'Thank you for the explanation, monsieur.'

Poireau questioned the bar steward, a wizened Cockney who

rattled off information without a second's pause in his polishing of glasses on the counter.

The answers were what Poireau had expected.

A simple problem, really – hardly worthy of his powers. Yet there remained something not quite right. One detail. . . .

Poireau put his little black notebook neatly into his pocket and sought out the Hon. Mrs Chip-Ebberly.

Mrs Chip-Ebberly, though burdened with a shawl, a rug, a knitting-bag, and a large handbag, refused to be seated. They stood, and kept their balance with some difficulty. As Poireau had expected, Mrs Chip-Ebberly was cold and brusque. But she was also agitated. Her eyes darted past him as if she feared the approach of an enemy.

On Poireau's reminder, she admitted that they had met some years previously. 'I thought that I knew your face. And, in fact, your name struck me as faintly familiar when I examined the passenger list.'

Poireau was vexed. He said: 'You are too kind, madame. I myself remember the circumstances well. I was instrumental in recovering some jewels for your brother. I trust his lordship is well?'

'Thank you.' Mrs Chip-Ebberly's mind was elsewhere. She jumped nervously as a steward passed.

Poireau said: 'They were exquisite diamonds. It would be a pleasure to feast the eyes on them again.'

Mrs Chip-Ebberly returned her attention to the little Belgian. She said repressively: 'They have been in the family for many years.'

One understood that this established their merit. Poireau sighed again. Never would he understand the British! He said: 'At present I am concerned with a very different case. And I should like to know madame, at what time you saw Miss Price come in from the deck last night.'

'At midnight precisely. I know because, being unable to sleep, I got up and left my cabin to check the clock in the Lounge, in order to put my watch back at the proper time.'

Poireau nodded sympathetically. An orderly mind, that! Already he had shuddered at the thought of the disastrous complications there might be, in determining alibis, on account of the changing of the clocks on the westward course.

To his surprise, Mrs Chip-Ebberly added: 'I do not think

41

that Miss Price had been murdering her uncle. It is not likely that a young niece would kill an uncle, however objectionable!'

Poireau regarded her with admiration. 'Not likely, *non, madame*,' he said gravely. He continued: 'And yet a short time ago you implied, I think, that this niece did do just that.'

Mrs Chip-Ebberly hesitated. She said: 'I now have reason to believe that *another* is guilty of the crime!'

Poireau's eyebrows rose invitingly. '*Oui, madame?*'

She said firmly: 'I intend to take the matter up with the Captain, in person!' Darkly she added: 'It is a case of *international espionage!*'

This time Poireau was really startled. He gazed at Mrs Chip-Ebberly with her swathings of wool and flannel, her rugs, her knitting. He said: 'This is, indeed, interesting!'

Mrs Chip-Ebberly looked about nervously again. It was as if she feared a spy at her shoulder. With a nod to Poireau, she departed.

Poireau shrugged. He sent a steward to ask the First Officer to arrange a meeting with Miss Price and Mr Homer T. Anderson.

Poireau announced: 'I have settled the question of Mademoiselle Price.'

Winifred Price looked at him with a curious intensity.

Anderson began to growl out something.

Poireau held up a cautionary finger. '*Doucement!*' he said. 'We have had enough of random recriminations. I do not accuse you, monsieur, of the murder. But you have told a lie. You have lied to Atlas Poireau!'

Anderson blustered: 'What are you talking about?'

Poireau said sharply: 'Yes! You lied when you said that Miss Price saw her uncle after you did. I recommend that, if you have spread that tale, you now take pains to correct it. You chatted with Mr Price last night. The topic of your conversation is not, at the moment, material. it was possibly, as you say, about the weather and the cuisine. About nothing at all! But in the course of this unimportant conversation Mr Price offers you a cigarette, which you accept.'

Poireau turned to Winifred. 'You mentioned that when you

spoke with your uncle, he had no cigarettes left? That was why he gave you none?'

She nodded.

Anderson said: 'So what? That only goes to prove what I said. He gave me a smoke, finished his packet, and then *she* came along.'

Poireau said: '*Non*, monsieur! The opposite is true. Mr Price was out of cigarettes when he spoke with his niece. When she left him he went below, bought two packets, and went on deck again – to talk with you! This I *know*. The bar steward recalls the purchase, just before the bar closed. We know Mr Price did not smoke all the cigarettes he bought, for they were found on his body – one packet still sealed, and one with five cigarettes gone. That was the packet he held out to you.'

'Then she's lying when she says he didn't have any when she was with him.'

Poireau shrugged. '*À quoi bon?* How could she know such a lie would help her? Moreover, there is a more conclusive proof. When Miss Price came to her uncle he had only a halfpenny left in English money: he told her so – and if you are sceptical of her account, monsieur, the steward recollects that when Mr Price paid for a cocktail just before dinner he put down a florin and had to make up the rest of the amount in American coins. Miss Price gave him two pound notes to exchange, she tells us. And in his pockets' – Poireau gestured dramatically towards the green box – 'we found English money to the amount of one pound, seventeen shillings, and a halfpenny – which would be the exact amount of change remaining to him after a purchase of two packets of cigarettes at one and sixpence each!'

Poireau looked about in triumph. He twisted his moustaches.

Anderson scowled. He said after a moment, grudgingly: 'Maybe I made a mistake. But I'm not talking any more without a lawyer.'

He went out.

The First Officer cried: 'Very pretty, Mr Poireau! Very neat! Though it is really quite obvious after all, isn't it, when one stops to think. There is the change, and there are the cigarettes – '

Poireau said noncommittally: 'Very obvious.'

Winifred Price still eyed him with a curious expression. She asked: 'Do you think Mr Anderson killed my uncle, Monsieur Poireau?'

'I do not know, mademoiselle.'

'Well, I – thank you,' she said.

Poireau looked at her a little sadly.

Winifred Price stood up suddenly. She said: 'Monsieur Poireau, you make me feel like a – you make me feel *anti-social!* And I don't understand. You've fooled Mr Anderson. Because he's stupid, and anyway he's scared about something. But you know very well you haven't been logical!'

Mr Waggish was shocked. He cried: 'Oh, I say, Miss Price!'

'*Non, mademoiselle?*'

'No! You proved I was with my uncle before Mr Anderson was. And because you exposed his lie that he saw me there later he wasn't cool enough, just now, to look critically at your argument. You haven't really proved . . . I could have gone up on deck again *afterwards, too*, couldn't I?'

'And you did so, *n'est-ce pas?* You went back on deck.'

Winifred said: 'Yes! I didn't go to bed when I told you I did. It's true about not seeing Uncle Paul again; but I went up to the boat-deck. It was midnight when I came in for good.'

Poireau nodded. 'And were seen by a witness.'

She gasped. 'You knew? You knew I lied about it? Then why did you believe me when I said I didn't kill my uncle?'

Poireau said: 'The witness said that you were the very picture of guilt, that your face was scarlet.'

'Then why – '

Poireau smiled. 'Mademoiselle, consider! The witness drew her own conclusions from what she saw. But then, she had not taken the course in psychology! Does one come in, when one has just killed a man and hidden his body – *blushing scarlet? Non!* One is pale. One trembles . . . But it is, on the other hand, extremely likely that one blushes in a different circumstance. If one had just had a rendezvous on the boat-deck!'

Winifred Price blushed. She said defensively: 'Well, I had to apologize for the way my uncle acted! And I was afraid

Tom would get into trouble if I told about meeting him on the boat-deck after dark. He said it was against the rules.'

Mr Waggish interposed: 'It surely is.' His eyes were round.

She said imploringly: 'It was my fault, Mr Waggish! And, Monsieur Poireau, you mustn't think I'm disloyal to Llewelyn! And anyway the Purser has a girl in Manchester.'

She left the room.

Mr Waggish said, 'I might have known Tom would be up to – So that was it!'

'*Oui. C'était ça.*'

Mr Waggish said doubtfully: 'I don't know French, Monsieur Poireau.' He added: 'But it certainly makes things sound more impressive!'

Poireau looked at him a little sharply. But the First Officer was innocent of irony. Poireau acknowledged: 'I have found it so.'

The door opened, and the Purser burst in. He cried angrily: 'I've just heard Miss Price is in trouble. They're saying she killed her uncle, just because she was seen on deck at midnight. But I can prove she was innocent. She was with me on – '

Mr Waggish said: 'She just told us about it. But Mr Poireau knew already. He found out by detecting!'

'She told – Oh!'

Poireau asked: 'You did not *know* she had told us, then?'

The Purser's very fair skin crimsoned. He clenched his fists, and retorted furiously: 'How *could* I know? No, I didn't!'

The First Officer said reassuringly: 'Mr Poireau has proved she is innocent.'

The Purser's anger vanished. He asked in surprise: 'You've already solved the crime, Mr Poireau?'

Poireau cried: '*Ah, non – par exemple!* Even Atlas Poireau requires more than an hour or two! The complications only now begin! Why does Anderson say nothing of his stolen cosh? What dastardly plot has Mrs Chip-Ebberly unconvered? Why did a pipe and a red and yellow muffler repose beneath the body?'

'It does sound mysterious.' Mr Waggish sounded pleased.

Poireau was pained. 'But', he declared, 'there is no such thing as "mystery", *mon cher*. There is only *disorder!* To solve a crime, is only to use the logic: to restore misplaced details to their proper position.'

Mr Waggish asked, a little taken aback at Poireau's vehemence: 'And the details that will not fit? that are illogical?'

Poireau said severely: 'In *my* cases there are no such things. I permit no nonsense! Life is *system*. One needs only to know the rules. Two and two make four. There are one hundred cents to a dollar. There are twenty shillings to a pound. Every action has a reaction. Every effect has a cause!'

The Purser nodded. He had calmed down. He said: 'As a mathematical man, I can appreciate that. Detecting must be like keeping books. You add this, you subtract that . . . Why, one could practically do it by machine! It's very simple.'

Poireau was piqued.

Mr Waggish shook his head. 'But could everyone *operate* such a machine? *I* saw the details. But *I* couldn't fit them into their proper places. I think it's wonderful what you've done, Mr Poireau!'

Atlas Poireau smiled modestly. He twirled his moustaches. He said: 'That is true!'

CHAPTER 5

SIR JON. NAPPLEBY

Death rays. Atom bombs. Hydrogen bombs.

> As if his whole vocation
> Were endless imitation.

Nappleby frowned. What on this paper he held – what in Price's history, that unedifying compound of the dull, the salacious, and the lucrative – what in Anderson's, grotesque and (it now appeared) sinister as well – could direct his subconscious mind to remembrance of a Wordsworthian and quasi-Platonic vision of childhood innocence?

He looked again at the printlike writing at the top:

> *Florabunda*. Capt. – *see*.
> And. 15gr?

and at the list below, written in a cruder, sprawling hand:

> Death rays
> A-bombs
> H. ”
> Moscow etc.
> genuine Imittation
> Kit? Bombinos

'This fell, you say, from Anderson's pocket?' Nappleby lifted a troubled gaze from the paper to the face of Mrs Chip-Ebberly, which emerged from a chaste chrysalis of sweaters, coats, and rugs.

'From his pocket. I could not help seeing what was written on it.' Mrs Chip-Ebberly paused to analyse her conduct. 'To be precise, I made no effort *not* to see what was written. Decorum was overmastered by some mysterious sixth sense. I read. Impelled, no doubt, by heredity.'

'Heredity?' Nappleby was uncertain.

'It was one of my forebears who discovered the scheme of the man Fawkes. Another Chip-Ebberly, under the Regency, foiled a plot to mine the Circumlocutions Office. It is scarcely to be wondered at, therefore, that I recognized this Anderson for what he is. I had already discovered that he was in possession of a dangerous weapon. He held mysterious conferences with Mr Price. When I found this paper, I desired to notify the Captain. But the First Officer informs me, Sir Jon., that *you* have had more experience of spies than the Captain has.'

'That is very interesting.' Nappleby was still more puzzled.

'It was my brother-in-law who prevented a Turkish agent from smuggling a sketch of the Albert Memorial out of the country. In *that* case, of course, the laws of heredity would not apply.'

Nappleby considered. 'Have you ever spoken with Anderson?'

'I have said good morning, or good evening, as the case might be. My object, of course, was to lure him on to betray himself. My cousin Fitz-Ebberly, who is with the Foreign Office, informs me that women are frequently used for such purposes in espionage, and, more to the point, in *counter*-espionage.' Mrs Chip-Ebberly adjusted a rug which threatened to slip from her shoulders. 'It is chilly here, but only on deck can one be sure of privacy ... In the foregoing connexion, I may observe that Mr Price was not infrequently in the company of a woman. A Miss Despana. The name can hardly be her own.'

Nappleby gave her the intelligent nod this innuendo seemed to require. 'And did you ever talk with Price himself?'

She arranged her rugs again, with extreme care, preparatory to moving. 'Certainly not.'

Nappleby sighed as she departed. One knew too much to dismiss her summarily as a crank. From just such freakish old ladies, from adolescents given to melodramatizing, from

timid house-agents' clerks, came information that was all too
real. This paper was real. Death rays ... Bombinos ...
endless imitation.

Again, why Wordsworth? The Della Robbian savour of
the conclusion might in some devious way have channelled
his memory. But no: that was not enough, any more than
was the puerile misspelling. *Imittation.* Nappleby sought help
in the poem itself:

Behold the Child among his new-born blisses,
A six years' Darling of a pigmy size!

See, at his feet, some little plan or chart,
Some fragment from his dream of human life,
Shaped by himself with newly-learned art ...

The rolling, the faint vibration, the creaking of the ship, as
Nappleby strode the deck, urged his thoughts ineluctably into
a different rhythm. The voice of some dim sub-analytical
stratum of his mind declaimed in jerking tempo:

A*las*, regard*less of* their *doom*
The *lit*tle *vic*tims *play*.
A*las*, regard*less of* their *doom*
The *lit*tle *vic*tims *play*.

No longer Wordsworth, even, but Gray. The bold catalogue
of horrors on the paper in his hand had led him, so far, merely
to a gallimaufry of gobbets from Augustan and Romantic
showpieces. Wordsworth would not have been pleased at the
jumble. He had called Gray gaudy and inane. Or rather
(a pained and scholarly Nappleby hastened to point out in
querulous emendation) had, in speaking of a particular poem
of Gray's –
· Nappleby recalled his wandering thoughts: there was, very
likely, no time for academic self-indulgence. Yet often enough
just such vagrancy, such a divagation from the superficially
relevant into allusion, reminiscence, quotations, had been the
very lifeblood of his triumphant investigations. A line from
Samuel Johnson: a pastiche of Swinburne: an obsessive

phrase from Horace, Ploss, or Thomas Tusser – any of these might prove an Archimedean lever.

But in *this* case? *Quid Christus Inieldo?* What had epiphanies of pure and ecstatic infancy to do with weapons of mass destruction? With, it might be, international intrigue – with some vast plot directed against metropoles?

In one sense, of course, the connexion was only too patent. The poet Gray, upon a Prospect of Eton College, had thought of death. Anyone might relapse into a far profounder melancholy now, at the thought of the modern Prospect noumenally as well as (Nappleby glanced out at the indeterminate grey seascape) phenomenally conceived. To think of children was to think, by way of the immediate past, of the hideous possible future. But so general and platitudinous an association of ideas was surely not sufficient . . . Nappleby frowned at the paper again. Certain details were puzzling. 'Kit' – why Kit? Christopher? Cat, kitten? Panther? A Boy Scout's duffelbag? Yet most of the details were clear in substance.

Nappleby thought of clues he had been grudgingly handed in other cases: vague, cryptic, lacunose. Whereas nothing would be more concrete and explicit than 'H-bomb'. The only uncertainty was what the whole thing was about . . .

Nappleby welcomed the approach of the First Officer. Mr Waggish scowled incredulously at the troublesome catalogue. 'Good God! Bombs? I thought the old girl was *daft* when I shoved her on to you!'

'I should be glad to know your interpretation of this paper.' Nappleby was adept in eliciting suggestions from the *verecund*.

Mr Waggish was different. 'There are two different handwritings.' He looked questioningly at the man from Scotland Yard.

'Yes. The neat hand is Price; the other, Anderson.'

'Ah?'

'The Purser was able to find a specimen of their handwritings for purposes of comparison. There is, I should judge, no question.'

'After all, I'm no' so entirely astonished, then, Sir Jon. Anderson is a rum cove. Very rum indeed. I told you what Mr. Poireau found about his lies! And so he's fouled up with atomic weapons!'

'But uncertain, apparently, about his target. Which may afford us a ray of hope. Or he is – possibly – concerned only with their manufacture and distribution, not with plots for their employment. You say he calls himself a man of business.'

'I've had Sparks radio ashore to ask about him.' Grimness overtaking incredulity, the First Officer frowned again. '*Spies* on this vessel!'

'What else do you deduce from this paper?'

'One other thing.' Mr Waggish was gaining assurance. 'It seems awfully outright. You'd expect code. That is, I thought spies always used secret language. Cryptograms, invisible ink, and so on. In stories, surely, they do!'

'In my experience too.' Nappleby cast his mind back. 'They try to make their activities seem commonplace, harmless, trifling.'

Yes: they dissimulated so elaborately that the dissimulation became a fine art though black. They were plausible, pretended to deal in belles-lettres, verses, paintings, *kick-shaws*. Always in time – and just in time – Nappleby had managed to cut through their poetastical frills and expose the truth. *This* time the frills, the *infuscation*, the periphery of childishness, were of his own providing; the actual *donnée* itself was stark, explicit, and horrible. Why then did he find himself ornamenting that naked list: find himself thinking of the conspirator as some giant Idiot-Boy (which was Words-worth again), some Brobdingnagian natural drooling and lolling with his bauble, settling the fate of the twentieth-century world quite without prejudice; order and distinction lost? (Genuine versus imittation; enemies – enemies versus God knew what!) Plucking off the petals of a daisy and chanting in innocent indifference 'New York, Moscow, New York, Moscow', towards the last petal, which would deter-mine which shall fall. *Urbs delenda est;* but which one? And what part had the ratlike Price played in all this? Was he in the plot, or had he met death because he threatened to publish it?

'Capt. – *see.*'

Was the *Florabunda* herself engaged in some Gargantuan plot, fantastic in its sheer gaucherie? – for if the conventional apparatus of espionage is trite, still it is gauche to ignore the conventions. Could one trust the Captain? Nappleby had seen a fanatic gleam in his eyes. For that matter, could one trust Mr Waggish himself?

With a sense of physical relief, gulping fresh air in after near-asphyxiation, Nappleby decided that here at least lay solid ground. The First Officer was no spy. His indignation was genuine; it carried, moreover, an overtone of unselfconscious boyish excitement which no conspirator could simulate, nor, indeed, have the refinement of imagination to desire.

Mr Waggish stood waiting now for the pearls of wisdom which an Assistant Commissioner of Scotland Yard must drop. In fact the First Officer's faith, Nappleby acknowledged with a sigh, put upon one a heavy responsibility. He asked his next question rather abstractedly: 'Does the name Thomas Gray suggest anything to you?'

'Aye!' Mr Waggish spoke promptly and apparently without being disconcerted by the tangential character of the inquiry. 'I know some of his poetry. "When you see three lights ahead, Right rudder, and show your red." And then there is "Green to green or red to red, Perfect safety, go ahead!" '

'Thomas Gray?'

'Gray'.

'Not the same man, I fancy.'

Mr Waggish shrugged. 'He is in *Standard Seamanship* – it's a very fine book. You'll know his "General Caution"?

> 'Both in safety and in doubt,
> Always keep a good look-out.
> In danger, with no room to turn,
> Ease her – stop her – go astern!'

'Your Gray sounds a practical man.' They had come to a bulkhead door leading in from deck; Nappleby paused. 'The "good look-out" is admirably to the point. We are certainly in doubt. But are we in danger? And if so, exactly how?'

The ship's Doctor joined them as they entered the cabin which was being used as headquarters.

'You are a poet, Doctor. Do you know Wordsworth's "Ode on Intimations of Immortality"?' Nappleby was still nagged by Wordsworth. Of course there was always, he thought, Spy Nosy . . .

The Doctor's face brightened. He took his pipe from his mouth and brandished it like a chunky baton. 'I once *wrote* an ode. To a tanker I sailed on once. In thirty-five stanzas it was, Pindaric, very beautiful! That was before I became interested in the heroic poem –

'Descend, Heroic Muse! Foresake Parnassus' hilly height
    For that sad plain where languishes Tipptop in sorry
        ploight:
Noble Tipptop, the valiantest –

Do you know, Sir Jon., how many lines I have written so far? Fifty-seven thousand! And it is not yet complete. You might like to hear part of it? Waggish has heard a bit, last night.'

'Aye, it's fine stuff.' The First Officer stooped to pick up an envelope that lay on deck just outside the cabin door.

The Doctor waved his pipe, eyes closed, in time to some delicious rhythm which beguiled his inner ear. 'You must listen to it, Sir Jon. We had an Oxford don aboard, three trips back, who heard the Invocation, and part of the first canto, and the descent to the underworld, and he was tremendously moved.' The Doctor's pudgy face quivered in all its parts with emotion recollected. 'He said the only English poet whom he could think of who gave a comparable experience was Sir Richard Blackmore!

'To see the Gods come down to earth and mortal men
    accost,
To see their spears hurled fore and aft, their faerie lances
    tossed,
I rate my life a gudgeon's worth, and count the World Well
    Lost!'

Mr Waggish had pulled something from his envelope. He gave a low cry. 'Gosh – look at this!'

Nappleby took the green slip he extended. 'Fifteen thousand dollars drawn on the Bank of New York and Washington, payable to Paul Price – signed by Homer T. Anderson.'

'Fifteen thousand dollars! That's – ' The First Officer broke off, round-eyed.

'Quite so. It is more than five thousand pounds. It is also, I fancy, what Price meant when he jotted "15 gr?" on that paper. A grand is a thousand. We can remove the interrogation point. Mr Anderson was apparently willing to pay up.'

'Blackmail?'

'It suggests itself. But for what?' Nappleby sat down, puzzled.

'Who put the cheque in here?' the Doctor displayed an unanticipated capacity for coming to the point.

'Anyone could have pushed it under the door, I suppose.' The First Officer spoke thoughtfully. 'But who *would* have done so except the killer? Will there be fingerprints, Sir Jon.?'

'Yours and mine, now. The person who put it here will have had the brain to remove his own. The envelope could have come from any writing-desk on the ship.'

'At least, it wouldn't have been Anderson who called it to our attention this way.'

'Anderson! There's a strange man.' The Doctor jabbed the air sagely with his pipe. 'I took him a seasickness pill the first day out; he must have not have heard me knock, for when I went in he was on his hands and knees, and ye'll never guess what he was doing.' The pipe hung poised between disgust and ridicule. 'He was playing with a doll! He thrust it out of sight, but not before I'd seen it.'

'If he's dotty, that simplifies things.' Mr Waggish was rather relieved than otherwise by this evidence of abnormality. 'Shall I send and have him put into the brig?'

The Doctor's eyes flashed in approbation:

' "Away with him," cried Sarazin. "Away to dungeon deep,
With toads and rats to languish there, nor may he hope to
    sleep!" '

Nappleby waited patiently for the last iamb to wend its limping way. 'Not yet. I shall follow Mr Price's schedule. "*Florabunda*. Capt. – *see*." '

The two officers exchanged a look of dubiety.

'Could someone do an errand *for* you?' The First Officer rubbed his chin.

'I had really better go myself.' Nappleby was mystified. 'I know it is not customary ... but surely under the circumstances – '

Mr Waggish screwed up his tanned face: unscrewed it after some tortuous ratiocinative process. He fixed a faintly hopeful blue eye on Nappleby. 'Were you by any chance in the Navy during the War, Sir Jon.?'

'I am afraid not. No. Why?'

'It might have helped. We had better say that you *were* in the navy. Or – no.' The First Officer sighed. 'Perhaps not. Mind you, he *may* be quite okay today.'

'But – '

'It's a little awkward to explain.' The First Officer led the way from the cabin as he spoke. 'You understand, *I* have no prejudice against landsmen. Some of my best friends live ashore. But the Old Man – well, he's a purist, if you take my meaning. If you'll just bear that in mind ... He's dotty, of course.'

'Ah.' Nappleby weighed this information. 'The Doctor is more broad-minded?'

'Oh, aye.'

'And more – balance?'

'Yes, he's a very fine chap. To be sure, you might call his poetry an obsession. Not that it doesn't have some very noble thoughts in it. "To see the Gods descent to earth di dum di dum di dum, I'd rate my life a something something, and hold the World Well Lost" – very noble!'

'A bit extreme, perhaps? That is, I gather that at that juncture of the fable his hero is prepared to liquidate his army and himself for the sake of seeing seraphim, or whatever, on the battlefield? Rather like Nero firing Rome for the sake of the spectacle.'

'Extreme?' Mr Waggish's repetition of this verdict was uncertain. His face cleared as he apprehended what he took to be the root of the criticism: 'Oh, of course there's no such thing really as gods and fairies and all that. But what I was driving at – the thoughts may be noble; but as to the – ah, the *literary merit* ...' Poised at the top of the companion, he turned a keen eye on Nappleby. 'What would you say, now, of this Sir Richard Blackmore he mentioned? Was he a celebrated writer?'

Nappleby phrased his reply meticulously. 'To call him merely obscure would be, I fear, to glorify him unduly. He was, in fact, one of the worst writers in the language. But voluminous. Oh, very voluminous.'

The First Officer nodded as at verification of a cherished but doleful hypothesis. 'Now if you'll just wait, Sir Jon., I'll tell the Old Man you are here.'

Perched high on the *Florabunda*, the Captain's quarters nevertheless suggested a cave – arched above, and gloomy in the pallid light of the foggy afternoon. A Homeric cavern, deep-sunken in the sea – but a sea neither wine-dark nor wine-heady, but perversely dull, throwing up a surly screen of grey.

A light snapped on, dispelling Nappleby's *speluncar* reverie. His sight of the Captain chased out Homer with an heroic charge of iambics: *With many a tempest had his beard been shaken* . . . Here (and this was in gratifying contrast to the Wordsworthian echoes still remotely troubling Nappleby) the process of association was copiously clear. But also – it was chastening to acknowledge – banal: the merest undergraduate would have found himself repeating the same line on beholding the Captain.

Yet the association was not wholly impractical. Chaucer's peregrinating Shipman had never struck out into the open Atlantic. His ship (*His barge ycleped was the Maudelayne*) – his *Magdalen*, which paid customs at Dartmouth in the 1360s, had not the labyrinthine engine-rooms of the *Florabunda* nor had she carried burlap sackfuls of advertisements, *billets-doux*, and copies of the London *Times* to a region beyond Ultima Thule. Yet the Shipman was the forerunner of this tall, green-eyed, deep-eyed mariner in navy and gold.

Hardy he was, and wise to undertake . . . but he had been, as well, a good bit of a scoundrel. Had the seafaring tradition in this respect changed as drastically as in its views on square rigs and keelhauling? Were the products of Pangbourne, and Kings Point, New York, now officers and gentlemen merely? Or were they still capable of bloody deeds? Had this Captain, in brief, dealt in murder like his medieval forebear?

If he had, Nappleby surmised, it was for more reward than a share in the cargo. Even for more than the pleasure of intrigue. It must be a matter of piracy on the grand scale, to judge from his countenance:

> His beard was long, his face was brown,
> And his eyes were wild.

But now quotation was degenerating into irresponsibility. Checking further quaint transmogrifications, Nappleby approached the Captain, whose eyes softened till they beamed with the mild graciousness of an autarch granting audience: which was, Nappleby reminded himself, no figure, but a literal denomination of the facts.

'My First Officer tells me that you're book-learned.' The Captain beckoned imperiously. 'What would you say to this, now? Do you know this book?'

Nappleby scrutinized the thick quarto which lay open to its title-page on the Captain's table. '*The Anatomy of the Ocean Sea?* I fear I am not familiar with it, sir.'

'Aye, *The Anatomy of the Ocean Sea: Its Nature and Tropes with the Severall Parts and the Creatures that Dwell Therein; declaring the Sovereignty of Sea-Men, and the secrets of the true Dominion of the World, with the opinion of Platon thereon fully and truthfully discovered.*'

The Captain placed enormous, orotund stress on every word of the title. Nappleby's gaze flickered about the cabin: to the bunk, the settee, the charts, the desk – on the desk, partly hidden by the quarto, was the picture of a woman with flowing hair, and near the picture stood a globe on which the seas, rife with arrows, ships, and dolphins, girdled blank and nameless continents.

' " . . . many strange places, waters, seas, straits, havens, channels, isthmuses, canals, and the waters below which afford fishes, whales, sea-monsters, mermaidens, remora, giant barnacles – " '

The Captain's finger kept his place on the yellowed page. 'This Platon, now – you know his name? He was a Greek, I take it? Aye . . . They're bad sailors, the Greeks. I've put into the Piraeus often. Dirty blighters; the vessels foul bottoms all of them. But let that be . . . This Platon says, as I take it, that material things are not real. They are only shadows. And the mind should not be fouled up in them.'

'That is, perhaps, a way of putting one aspect of Plato's thought.'

'The mind ought to command the machine?'

'It would be easier to give an opinion in a specific case.' Nappleby was cautious.

'Aye. Well, look here.' The Captain patted his beard. His strange eyes wavered. He seemed, suddenly, almost shy. 'According to the engineers, my ship will do twenty-one knots, if pressed.'

'Ah?'

'It's a simple matter – on the material plane, that is.' The Captain sighed. 'You take your r.p.m., times 60, times the pitch of the propeller, times the slip, all over 6,080, and you get your speed.'

'I see.'

'Aye. That gives you your knots. But' – the Captain removed his hand from his beard to thump the table – 'if material things are not real, who is to say she can do only twenty-one knots? Why should the Queens do more? or' – the Captain winced – '*the United States?* Why should not *I* have the Blue Riband? Why should I be bound by mere illusion – '

Nappleby thought it best to take a firm stand. 'In such a case I should be guided by the engineers. The scientists. There are limits to the power of the will, in the sphere of becoming, at least.'

'I dare say.' The Captain heaved another melancholy sigh. But as he stared down at his book a wanchancy glint, stubborn and secretive, returned to his eyes.

'Besides, is speed so important, sir?' Nappleby was soothing. 'If one wants to hurry, one can travel' – he took care to voice disdain – 'by air.'

'Air! 'Tis only b–s like that lubber who got his this morning who would travel by air.'

'Do you know why he was killed?' Nappleby flung the question out abruptly.

'Of course. He was killed because he insulted the *Florabunda*.'

'Ah.' By an acrobatic exercise of the imagination, Nappleby followed the Captain's logic – for possibly it was logical, granted certain assumptions, to suppose that Price had been punished by some avenging Triton; by the sacred horses of Poseidon, plunging inexorably up out of the waves. 'Quite so. But there was a human agent involved. Price was struck on the back of the head.'

'That may be.' The Captain was courteous but indifferent.

Nappleby reverted to direct interrogation. 'Do you know who that agent was, sir?'

'No. Ask my First Officer. He said he would investigate. He must know by now.'

'He is investigating. But it is not easy to find out who, of all the persons involved, snatched three minutes unobserved at that hour of night. It could have been anyone. Everyone moves about so freely.'

'Ha!' Nappleby had touched another raw sore. 'It all comes of catering to passengers. In the old days you kept landlubbers below, in the hold; you battened down the hatches; you kept them out of the way till they could be unloaded. They fed on bread and water. But now! They wamble about from stem to stern. Cinemas! Dancing! Wireless! We even have to carry women. Human women!'

Nappleby, mildly intrigued by this special view of maritime history, was particularly caught by the concluding epithet, which the Captain mouthed with extraordinary verjuice; it was (Nappleby guessed) a mere tautology like 'moral man' or (more apposite) the Peggotty family's 'drowned dead'. And now, he realized, the Captain had swung back to metaphysics, to voice a private dualism:

'There's right and there's wrong. There's sea and there's land. You cannot have it both ways.'

'And Price was a landsman. Yes. Incidentally, it seems that he intended to pay you a visit, sir. Did he do so?'

'*Visit me?*' The Captain's expression rendered further working of the point superfluous.

'There is the possibility also' – Nappleby was deliberately circuitous – 'that his death may be connected with a plot involving high explosive weapons – '

'What?' The Captain's face was contorted; his eyes shot flame. 'He brought *explosives* aboard the *Florabunda?*'

'No, no. I should say there's no present peril. And it was not Price who was plotting for their use, but another passenger; Price appears to have found out about it. The object of the attack is apparently Moscow, or possibly New York; the conspirators, if that is what they are, seem to be above taking sides.'

'Oh – cities.' The Captain shrugged. He sat down, relieved. 'I don't suppose any of your officers would be involved in such doings? They are all trustworthy?'

'They spend their leaves ashore.' The Captain's beard trembled again, but more in sorrow than in anger. 'With human women.' He relapsed into a despondent meditation upon the botchedness of modern civilization which left little scope for the conversational amenities. Nappleby withdrew with a final glance at the charts, the globe, the *Anatomy of the Ocean Sea*, and the picture. He could now see this last item entire. The face was indeed lovely; and – *mulier formosa superne* – the torso ended in a finny tail.

The Captain's whereabouts at the time of Price's death ought perhaps to be ascertained. But the Captain was innocent of trifling with atomic warfare. If he had no love for the kingdoms of the earth, he would rely for their destruction on the powers of Neptune. He would simply await another Deluge.

Nor was *Anderson* himself dealing in total annihilation. Nappleby laughed as he swung down the lurching companion. The interlude above, lubricating his mind, had shown him how to fit Anderson into place. And the significance of Wordsworth's 'Ode'.

But Anderson might still, of course, be the murderer.

'You were gone a long while.' Mr Waggish eyed him protectively. 'Did you see what I meant?'

Nappleby nodded. 'Mania of a rather uncommon variety. Thalassophilia. Or ought I say "tellurophobia"?' He regarded the First Officer's ingenuous face with some compunction. 'I should say, better yet, that he hates the land and adores the sea.'

The First Officer shook his head respectfully at the apology implicit in the last remark. 'It's a privilege to hear you, even if I don't always understand, Sir Jon. Anybody can tell you're an educated man.'

'I suppose' – Nappleby experienced a recrudescence of

anxiety – 'that the Chief Engineer is aware of the Captain's – idiosyncrasy?'

'Oh, the engineers are all dotty.' Mr Waggish proffered this equivocal reply (which Nappelby found distinctly barren of reassurance) with unshadowed cheerfulness, as prelude to a query of his own. 'Now what, Sir Jon.? Anderson?'

'Anderson. The time has come, I fancy, to tackle him. We must have a little *éclaircissement*.'

Mr Waggish remembered something as they made their way above. 'Whilst you were with the Old Man, Anderson tried to get into Price's cabin. There's a man on guard whilst Inspector Tourneur searches the room. When he was challenged Anderson pretended he'd mistaken the door, and went away. That's suspicious, is it not?'

'It is. Though if he killed Price, why is he waiting so long to go to his cabin to cover his traces, if that was his intention?'

'There he is now.' Mr Waggish indicated a bulky form at the rail. As he spoke Anderson turned to face them warily.

'This paper is in your writing, is it not?' Nappleby held up the cheque for him to see, without preliminaries.

Mr Waggish's warning cry was too late: Anderson's spatulate fingers seized the cheque with greater speed than they seemed capable of, and flung it out to sea; he emitted a gross and exultant grunt.

With a mocking swish the wind blew the cheque back, fluttered it in coquettish derision against his conoid nose, loosed it, and tossed it against a bulkhead, whence Mr Waggish retrieved it deftly.

Anderson's eyes bulged; his jowls quivered; he appeared reduced to a gelatinous state by what he must have considered a wanton flouting of Newtonian protocol.

'The first law of the sea, Mr Anderson.' The First Officer viewed him equably. 'Never spit to windward.'

The signs of some inner agitation were visible upon the triangular countenance as upon the face of some squat and putty-coloured metronome whose works had suddenly gone on the blink. Anderson gibbered. 'I didn't kill Price! It was a legitimate business deal!'

Mr Waggish turned red with moral indignation. Nappleby placed a restraining hand on his arm, and said: 'In that case, you will not object to our examining your cabin.'

'But . . .' Anderson's protest died as he looked from the First Officer's outraged face to Nappleby's implacable one. He grunted again, but this time in acquiescence – an acquiescence at first grudging and vengeful, but then displaying, in nicely graded succession, tinges of willingness, eagerness, excitement, pleasure, and triumphant pride.

'He may have some dirty trick up his sleeve.' Mr Waggish held Nappleby back as Anderson turned to conduct them below. 'There may be a booby trap – some bloody gadget – '

'I fancy we are in no danger.' Nappleby started calmly after the titubating financier. '*Pabulum*, pap for babes, Mr Waggish.'

In emulation of this nonchalance the First Officer lit a cigarette; he deposited his match in a sandbox with a hand that shook a little.

Anderson dragged a heavy foot-locker from under his berth. He unlocked it and put the cover back. His head and shoulders cut off their view of his actions: a clanking sound suggested the withdrawal of nameless metallic objects.

'There!' Still on his haunches, Anderson moved aside at last.

On the deck was spread a miniature city: ships, towers, domes, theatres, and temples, based on plastic, lay open to the grey light seeping through the porthole; a factory and a school, a park and a roundabout. At right and left were tall pylons, with a silver wire hanging between them. Anderson's finger touched a button, and the roundabout revolved to the tinkling of 'Three Blind Mice'; a troop of inch-high soldiers marched stiffly out of a redbrick barracks, halted, turned, and marched back in again.

'Look!' Anderson had forgotten his troubles in a concentration of glee. He delved into the trunk again, and brought out a model aeroplane: this he attached to the wire near the right-hand pylon. 'Bang, bang!' he muttered absorbedly; pressing a second button. The plane slid along the wire. There was another, louder *Bang*, a genuine crash 'embowled with outragious noise the aire', and a huge cloud of white dust billowed up, powdering the tweed jacket of Nappleby, the dark twill of Mr Waggish. As the dust cleared, and the smoke, they beheld a heap of whitish fragments, the residuum of the bustling metropolis.

Anderson tore his eyes from this feast to view his guests. 'How do you like that? Better than popguns, hey?'

'Good God!' Mr Waggish brushed ineffectually at his uniform. The door opened to reveal the pale face of a steward and the nozzle of a fire-hose; Mr Waggish waved them out again.

'How's that?' Anderson beamed in sanguinolent tripudiation.

'Incredible.' Nappleby was succinct.

'Of course, this is only a rough model. There is room for improvement. The beauty of it is, the bomber can be used over and over, but the buildings are only guaranteed for one game; then the kids have to get replacement kits at three-fifty per.'

'They have their choice of cities – London, Paris, New York?'

'They – Say! What do you think I am, a Red? This is a legitimate business deal.'

'This is, I suppose, the Kiddie Kit.'

'No!' Anderson was contemptuous. 'That's what we call the junior size – no real explosion, just marbles fall out of the bomb-door and knock the houses down. We use a farmhouse in the Kiddie Kit – two cows, a pig, a bunch of hens.'

'You hadn't thought of supplying toy corpses?'

'In the Superset you get Mother, Father, Sister, Brother, plus the soldiers, *plus* an extra set of A-bombs. Then – ' Anderson directed a suddenly distrustful and comminatory look at his visitors. 'You understand this is all on the Q.T.! The patent's pending. When we get manufactured in quantity we break out with a big advertising campaign. Radio! TV!'

Mr Waggish found voice at last. 'You'll hand the whole bloody mess over to me this minute. And' – he checked an outraged yell on Anderson's part – 'you can stow the gaff! Or rather' – Mr Waggish changed his mind – 'you can explain that cheque to us.'

Anderson glowered, Caliban torn from play. He was defiant. 'I won't talk without a lawyer. I guess I know my rights.'

'Your *rights!*' Mr Waggish swallowed.

For the second time, Nappleby prevented an outburst. He

led the First Officer into the passageway. 'We may as well wait. Commandeer his toys by all means. But he is not a spy.'

'And I thought he was our villain!' Mr Waggish had not yet recovered his equanimity. He sighed.

'Of course, one may choose to regard, what he is doing as atrocious enough. On the whole I prefer some spies I have known.'

'And we still don't know why he gave Price a cheque for fifteen thousand dollars – for blackmail or whatever!'

'Any lawyer will tell him to say he paid Price for help in advertising his little games. He may even think of saying so himself.'

Mr Waggish was struck by this suggestion. 'It might even be true.' He frowned dubiously. 'Do you think he killed Price, Sir Jon.?'

'I don't know.'

'And how did you discover what he was up to?' Mr Waggish seemed to remember something: 'Did you use logic, and simply put misplaced details into place in the proper system?'

'It was rather a matter of pursuing certain themes from Wordsworth and Gray.'

The First Officer was wistful. 'It must be hard to be a detective unless one reads a great deal of poetry?'

'It is difficult to solve a case without a thorough knowledge of the classics and of modern European literature.' Nappleby considered. 'Indeed, I suspect that crime and *indagation* are not only inherently arcane, fantastic, and polysyllabic, but quintessentially allusive.'

Mr Waggish sighed. 'Well – I should like to put Anderson into the brig; but since you say not' – he brushed ineffectually at the powder on his trousers – 'we had better go and change our clothes.'

CHAPTER 6

JERRY PASON

Jerry Pason hummed to himself as he knotted his tie before the mirror on his cabin wall.

There was a knock on the door.

'Come in!' Jerry Pason called.

The door opened. A large, heavy man with a conic-shaped head appeared. He wore a worried, nervous expression.

'You're Jerry Pason?' he asked.

'That's right,' Pason said.

'I'm Homer T. Anderson,' the big man said.

'I know,' the lawyer said. 'I've seen you about the ship. What can I do for you, Mr Anderson?'

'I want a lawyer,' Anderson told him. 'I hear you're a good one. I've been trying to get hold of you for hours.'

Pason said: 'I've been busy. Sit down, Mr Anderson.'

Anderson sat down, wiping his forehead. He gazed anxiously at Pason.

Pason said, 'Have a cigarette.'

Anderson's puffy hands shook as he took one from the packet Pason held out. Pason lit the cigarette. Anderson said: 'I'm a rich man, Mr Pason. I'll pay anything – anything!'

The lawyer raised his hand. 'One moment, Mr Anderson.' He pressed a button marked 'Steward'.

When the steward put his head into the room Jerry Pason told him: 'Ask my secretary, Miss Deet, to come with her notebook.'

Anderson protested: 'I don't want anyone else in on this.'

'You'll have to let my secretary hear it,' the lawyer said, 'or go elsewhere for counsel.'

There was another knock on the door. The door opened. Stella Deet came in.

'You wanted me, Chief?' she asked.

'We have a client,' Pason told her. 'This is Mr Homer T. Anderson. You remember I told you he might run into trouble.'

'You knew I'd come to you?' Anderson demanded.

'Just a hunch,' Pason said enigmatically.

Stella Deet sat down, crossed her shapely legs, propped her shorthand notebook on one knee, and waited with her pencil poised in the air.

Anderson blurted out: 'I'm afraid I'm going to be arrested for the murder of Paul Price.'

Pason said suavely, 'Oh?' He raised his eyebrows.

Anderson gasped, 'You know about it?'

'I want to hear you tell about it,' Pason said noncommittally.

'I didn't kill him!' Anderson said, wiping his forehead. 'But things are piling up against me. I tried to keep a certain business deal secret, so I made some misstatements. The people who are investigating know I talked with Price last night, and so far nobody has been found who saw him later. They found a cheque I gave him for fifteen thousand. But I didn't kill him!'

'Start from the beginning,' Pason said crisply. 'How long have you known Price-'

'Only since coming aboard. I never saw him before that.'

'And was it just coincidence that brought you on the same ship?'

'Yes.' Anderson licked his mouth nervously. 'Just coincidence.'

'You're sure?' Pason asked sternly.

Stella Deet darted an alert, inquisitive look at the businessman.

'I – '

'I can't help you unless you tell the truth,' Pason told him. 'You needn't be afraid. This is a privileged conversation. But you must be honest with me. I think you're lying now. I saw you with Price the first night out, and it certainly looked to me as though you were doing your best to make his acquaintance – as if you'd come on purpose for that!'

Stella Deet's pencil flew over the pages of her shorthand notebook. Her eyes went to Pason in poignant admiration.

'Well,' Anderson said reluctantly, 'the fact is, I sailed on this ship because I heard Price would be on board.'

'You must have wanted to meet him pretty badly,' Pason said.

Anderson said glibly: 'I have a new product coming out. I was anxious to have Paul Price give it publicity in his newspaper column.'

Stella Deet darted another alert, suspicious glance at him. She looked sidelong at Pason.

Pason asked: 'What is this product? What's your company?'

Anderson told them pompously: 'I have lots of companies. This one is the Merry-O Novelty Company. It is a subsidiary of General Metals, of which I am a director! We have a series of children's games coming out: a death-ray kit, an A-bomb kit, and so on. The patents are pending. I had a sample kit in my cabin I'd show you, only the First Mate stole it from me.' Anderson's voice rose. His face turned purple.

'Take it easy,' the lawyer said mollifyingly. 'Let's get the facts straight. You say you had this game, and you wanted publicity. Well, that seems harmless enough. Was that why you chased Price around the ship?'

'Yes, that's why.'

'Why were you so frightened?'

'Who says I was frightened?' Anderson demanded belligerently.

Pason looked at him with a level gaze. He let the subject drop. 'Well, what happened next?' he asked coolly.

'Last night I finally persuaded Price to say he'd write the game up, for fifteen thousand dollars. But he was alive when I left him! I tell you – '

'I want the details,' Pason said quietly. 'Where did you have this talk? When? What was said?'

'On deck, near where they found the body. It was about eleven-thirty or eleven-forty. I left at ten to twelve. I looked at my watch.'

'All right,' said Pason. 'Go on.'

'He agreed to write a plug in his column. I said I'd make out a cheque right off and bring it up to him, but he said to take it to his cabin because he'd be there soon, he had an appointment there at twelve-thirty.'

'Who with?' Pason asked sharply.

'He didn't say. That's all. He gave me a cigarette. He mentioned his niece, how she was a nuisance to him. He said it was a profitable trip. He laughed and said something screwy about how he hated the water except for the ice.'

'Do you know what he meant by that?' asked Jerry Pason.

'No.'

'And that was all?'

'Yes. I went down and made out the cheque. I knocked at his door, but there was no answer; so I slipped the cheque under the door in an envelope. It was about twelve-ten. That Scotland Yard dick has the cheque now – or the First Mate.'

'This may help establish the time,' Pason said thoughtfully. 'If Price did not keep his twelve-thirty appointment it was probably because he was already dead. If he did keep it he must have gone out on deck again later.'

Stella Deet asked, 'Isn't it suspicious that the person he was supposed to meet hasn't come forward, Chief?'

Pason smiled. 'Not necessarily. The person might be innocent of murder but have some reason for concealment. For instance, it might be a woman.'

'He was playing around with that actress, Dolores Despana,' said Anderson.

'Did he tell you she was the person he had a date with?'

'No,' Anderson admitted.

The lawyer asked him: 'Well, why is all this so damaging for you?'

Anderson cleared his throat. He said: 'Well, it wouldn't be except that I denied having any dealings with Price. And then I tried to dispose of the cheque by throwing it overboard. Also when I heard about the murder I went to his cabin to get the cheque back, and I was seen.'

Pason said: 'It may interest you to know that I have already heard about this cheque from the First Mate, and he did not find it in Price's cabin. Someone else took it from the cabin, and put it where the investigators would be sure to see it!'

Anderson stared at him. He looked terrified. He did not speak.

'Have you told me everything you know?' Pason asked him grimly.

'I – Yes!'

'Well,' Pason told him, 'I'll see what I can do. I'll get in touch with you. Meanwhile, don't talk unless I'm present.'

Anderson went out.

Stella Deet looked at Jerry Pason with secretarial solicitude. 'Chief,' she said tenderly, 'this is your vacation!'

'If he needs my help, that's what I'm a lawyer for,' Jerry Pason said, smiling.

'Do you believe him, Chief?'

The lawyer frowned. 'Half and half, Stella. I believe about half what he says, and I don't believe the other half. He's already thrown a lot of lies about. He wouldn't be in a mess if he'd told the truth about seeing Price. You notice he hasn't told us about the blackjack someone stole from him, or about how he tried to get Winifred Price into trouble. And there's more behind that cheque than payment for publicity. He's high up in a big concern. He's a director of General Metals, after all. Men like that don't usually handle advertising themselves. Remember, when we saw him chasing after Price, he was scared. My guess is, Price had something on him!'

'Blackmail!' Stella Deet exclaimed.

The lawyer smiled, nodded. 'It's what you'd expect. You know Price's reputation. Well, we have some questions to work on. Who gave that cheque to the First Mate? Certainly Anderson did not. It was completely against his interests.'

'A frame?' Stella Deet asked with quick intelligence.

Pason said: 'It could be. A clumsy frame. Extemporaneous. The whole thing strikes me, Stella, as unplanned. Sometimes that's the hardest kind of case to crack. Another question: Whom did Price expect to meet?'

He frowned. 'I wish we knew exactly when the killing took place.'

'It's too bad,' Stella Deet smiled, 'that the two old ladies I heard were on the wrong side of the ship!'

Pason looked up. 'What was that?'

'Oh, they were in the Lounge. Two little old ladies in old-fashioned clothes, very timid and quiet. Everyone was gossiping about the murder, of course, and one of these ladies said they'd heard a funny noise outside their window last night, like something being dragged. But that was on the port side, and Price was found to starboard.'

'Was one of them Lady Chip-Ebberly?'

'Oh, no. She is very stately and dignified. These were just two old ladies in rather countrified clothing. Besides, they were Americans. I could tell by the way they spoke. They didn't have English accents. Why, do you suspect her, Chief?'

'I wouldn't say that,' the lawyer told her. 'Only I've noticed her give Anderson some queer looks. And she seemed interested in Paul Price, too. I wouldn't put it past her to frame Anderson. Would you know those two old women again if you saw them?'

'Of course,' Stella Deet said. 'But how can they fit in?'

'Keep an eye out for them,' Pason told her. 'When you've located them, let me see them. You might – '

The door opened. Anderson burst in. He was puffing, and his eyes were bulging. He fell on to a chair.

Stella Deet seized a glass from the table. She went into the bathroom. She turned on the water, filled the glass, and handed it to Homer T. Anderson. He drank it.

'I knew I was being framed!' he gasped.

'What has happened?' Jerry Pason was tense but controlled.

Anderson put his hand into his pocket, came out with a blackjack. He put it dramatically down before Pason.

Pason leaned forward keenly. He examined the weapon. It showed distinct traces of blood.

'Where did this come from?' he asked calmly.

'It's mine!' Anderson cried. 'It was stolen from me before the murder, and now someone has planted it in my cabin!'

'You didn't mention owning a blackjack before,' Pason said, significantly.

'Because I hoped nobody would remember! I only got it as a souvenir. I collect murder weapons. I showed it to some people in the Lounge. I forgot to get it back afterwards. I haven't seen it since.'

'You're a fool,' Pason told him. 'We've known about your owning it all along. Who stole it from you that night?'

Anderson shook his head. 'I don't know. I'd had a drink or two – '

'Well put your mind to it,' Pason told him. 'Who on board this ship wants to get you into trouble?'

'Why, no one! I don't know anyone on board!'

'Someone seems to know you,' Pason said dryly. He got up, picking up the weapon. 'Now I want to see your cabin.'

'What are you going to do, Chief?' Stella Deet whispered as they followed Anderson along the passageway.

'To try and verify his story.'

'He seems genuinely frightened,' Stella Deet said.

The lawyer nodded as they entered Anderson's cabin. He asked, 'Where did you find the blackjack, Mr Anderson?'

Anderson pointed to the bed. 'Between the mattress and the wall.'

'The window was open as it is now?'

'Yes.'

Pason said, 'Wait here.' He picked up an ash-tray and went out.

Stella Deet and Homer T. Anderson stood silent as Pason left. Three minutes elapsed. Then the ash-tray was hurled in through the window. Anderson jumped, wiped his forehead. The tray landed on the bed and slipped down into the space between the mattress and the wall.

'Nice shot, Chief!' Stella Deet said when Pason returned.

'Just a little test. That's how the blackjack got here. Anyone passing along the deck outside the open window could have tossed it in. It must have happened since the berths were made up this morning, or the steward would have noticed it.'

'Get rid of it!' Anderson demanded. 'I would have thrown it overboard only I couldn't, because this window opens on the deck.'

'It's lucky you didn't,' Pason said. 'It would have been smarter to leave it right where you found it. Now it has your prints.'

Pason wiped the blackjack with his handkerchief. He removed the ash-tray and put the blackjack in its place. Then he scribbled a note and rang for the steward. He told the steward to take the note to the First Officer.

Stella Deet raised her eyebrows.

'We'll play along with the framer,' Pason said grinning. 'I'm only restaging the plant.'

'But – ' blustered Anderson.

'You just do as I say.'

71

The First Officer came and looked inquiringly at Pason, Anderson and Stella Deet.

Pason said: 'Mr Anderson is my client now. He found this blackjack here a little while ago. It is in the exact place where it would be if it had been thrown in by someone walking past the window. Someone threw it in to incriminate him.'

The First Officer looked at the window and the bed. He nodded. Pason picked up the blackjack in his handkerchief and showed it to him.

The First Officer asked: 'Isn't that your cosh, Mr Anderson? It looks like one you had in the Lounge.'

Anderson licked his lips. Sweat came out on his forehead. He looked over at Pason.

Pason said: 'My client concedes ownership. But it was stolen from him. He hasn't seen it since the night he had it in the Lounge.'

The First Officer asked: 'Why didn't he tell us about it earlier? Why, it must be the murder weapon! And why wasn't it thrown overboard?'

'It was kept,' Pason said, 'so as to frame my client.'

'Can we be sure it is the weapon?' Stella Deet asked.

'We can have it tested,' Pason said.

'I'll take it to the Doctor now,' said the First Officer.

Stella Deet and Jerry Pason accompanied him to the Doctor's office.

The First Officer asked, 'Can you be certain Mr Anderson is not pretending to frame himself?'

Pason smiled, said suavely: 'That's an improper question. But, off the record, I don't think he'd have the brains to try anything that complicated.'

The Doctor looked up impatiently from his desk.

Pason asked, 'Is it your opinion that this is the blunt instrument responsible for Paul Price's death?'

The Doctor looked at the blackjack. He said, 'It might be.'

'Will you test the blood? And look for hairs?'

The Doctor said grudgingly: 'All right. I'll let you know the results later. I'm a very busy man.' He bent to his desk.

Stella Deet asked as they went out, 'Do you like poetry, too, Mr Waggish?'

'Not my line, Miss Deet. I'm more a man for detective

stories – especially the ones with beautiful women assistants,' the First Officer told her smilingly.

Stella Deet laughed, blushed.

The First Officer went below. Pason and Stella Deet walked along the passageway.

'You know, Chief,' Stella Deet said thoughtfully, 'there's something funny about that Doctor. He seems more interested in something else than his medicine. He seems more interested in his poetry. In fact, the whole ship is funny. The Captain is said to be a maniac!'

'And the First Mate!' Pason smiled.

'Oh, he's terribly good-looking. And I love his accent!' Stella Deet said gaily.

'Better than an American one?'

'Not better than a California accent,' Stella Deet said softly.

'Stella . . .'said Jerry Pason. He took her hand.

A passenger came by. Pason let go Stella Deet's hand.

Stella Deet sighed. 'I'll go type up my notes, Chief,' she said.

Jerry Pason entered the Lounge. Two white-haired women in a corner caught his eye. One wore a brown cardigan and one a blue cardigan. They both wore high buttoned boots. Pason frowned, smiled. He made his way towards them. He fell into conversation with them.

'You're Americans?' he asked.

'Oh, yes,' said the old lady in the brown cardigan. 'We're on our way home.'

'I don't know *how* the *English* travel,' marvelled the other old lady. 'My goodness they are only allowed to take fifty pounds out of the country. Don't you think that's hard, Mr Pason?'

'You know my name?' asked the lawyer.

'Oh, everyone knows you! It's so terrible,' quavered the old lady in the brown cardigan. 'We've never been so close to a crime before. This morning when we heard about this terrible thing I told Lucinda it must have been the noise we heard.'

'But you know it couldn't have been, Letty,' the other old lady said firmly.

'What sort of noise was it?' Pason showed only polite, casual interest.

'Like something heavy being tugged and something wooden being rattled a little.'

'It wasn't just the creaking of the ship?'

'Oh, no, Mr Pason! I was nervous and asked Letty if she heard it too, and did she think someone was trying to get into our cabin through the window. We insisted on a cabin on A-deck, but now I see it has disadvantages!'

'Did you look out of the window?' the lawyer asked.

'Oh, no,' said the first old lady. 'We were both too seasick. That's why we were awake at such an hour, twelve-fifteen. I remember looking at my watch and wondering if I'd ever feel better. The watch has a luminous dial.'

Pason said politely, 'I hope you're better now?'

'Oh, yes. The Doctor came and gave us such wonderful pills!'

Pason asked sharply: *'Who's that looking in the window on the port side?'*

The two white heads turned promptly to starboard.

'Why,' said the second old lady, 'I don't see anyone there!'

'He's gone now,' Pason said.

He rose, bowed, said, 'Thank you!'

In the doorway he met Stella Deet.

'Those are the old ladies I told you about, Chief!' she told him in a quick, low voice.

The lawyer smiled. 'I know. And they're the biggest help we've had so far. They heard the murderer hiding Price's body under a tarpaulin outside their window at 12.15 a.m.!'

'But their cabin is on the other side of the ship!'

'Is it?' the lawyer grinned. 'That's what they think! Try them out, and you'll find they're wrong.'

'Chief how did you guess?'

'Well,' Pason told her, 'it wasn't likely that there would be two similar disturbances at the same time of night on exactly opposite sides of the ship. And many people, especially old people, don't really know port from starboard. It was a psychological probability.'

Stella Deet gazed at him in wistful adoration. 'How does it affect our client?' she asked.

'I think a little high pressure is in line,' Jerry Pason told her. 'Play up to me, Stella!'

He knocked at the door of Anderson's cabin.

74

Anderson opened the door. He let them in. He was too excited to bother with the formality of asking them to be seated.

'Well?' he asked eagerly.

'You've got to come clean,' Pason told him. 'I'm not going to work with a client who doesn't tell me the truth, the whole truth, and nothing but the truth.'

'I don't know what you're talking about.'

Jerry Pason told Stella Deet, 'You can send off that radiogram at once.'

'Right, Chief!' Stella Deet started for the door.

Anderson put his back against the door. He demanded, 'What radiogram?'

'To New York. They will be interested in knowing what Price had found out about your business in England.'

Anderson turned white. He gasped, 'You know?'

'I know plenty,' the lawyer said meaningfully.

Anderson fell on to a chair. He was panting. After a minute he asked, 'If you know, why do you insist on my telling the whole truth?'

'I want the satisfaction of hearing it from you,' Pason said coldly. 'That cheque wasn't to pay for advertising, was it?'

Anderson's resistance collapsed. He said: 'No. Not exactly. I was in England, see, and there was this chance to work a deal with a British firm. It would have meant millions! Only it didn't go through. That would have been the end of it, no harm done, only somehow or other Paul Price heard about the negotiations. He had spies everywhere! He telephones me in London to say he was going to run a story about it in his column.'

'And you didn't want your associates back home to find out,' Pason nodded.

'My God! They'd ruin me if they knew!' Anderson wiped perspiration from his face.

'So you followed Price on this ship to buy him off?'

'That was what he really wanted,' Anderson said.

'Blackmail,' the lawyer said significantly.

'What else could I do?' Anderson asked defensively.

'Well, what evidence did Price have?' Pason asked. 'He must have given you something besides his word, in exchange for fifteen thousand dollars.'

'No; it was mostly just what he'd heard,' Anderson said. 'He didn't need written proof. He did have a sheet of paper I'd made some notes on, and he made some notes of his own on it. He gave it back to me when I agreed to pay, but it wasn't vital at all. I had to take his word.'

'Where is it now?' Pason pressed him.

Anderson said angrily: 'The First Mate has it. I don't know how he got it. Someone must have picked my pocket.'

Pason looked at him in silence again.

Anderson shifted uneasily. 'But I didn't kill Price! I was framed!' His voice rose hysterically.

Jerry Pason rose.

'You'll help me?' Anderson gasped.

'We'll see,' said Pason.

Jerry Pason and Stella Deet went out.

'Gosh, Chief! What a colossal bluff!' laughed Stella Deet.

Pason grinned. 'He just had a guilty conscience. For a moment, I didn't know if it would work. It's a good thing I wasn't in court! Well, I think we've got down to rock bottom with him. I guessed when he mentioned General Metals he was afraid his associates would find out he'd been up to something on his trip abroad.'

'What comes next, Chief?'

'A drink,' Pason told her. 'We let Anderson stew in his own juice for a while.'

'My advice,' Jerry Pason told Homer T. Anderson, 'is that you let me tell Mr Waggish the whole truth.'

'What!' Anderson jumped up. He was still pale. 'Let me explain,' Pason said calmly. 'This is not an ordinary case. Nobody on board cares what crooked deal you tried to engineer in England. But if the case is not solved by the time we dock you will be questioned by the New York police, and all the facts will come out. There will be as much publicity as if Price had run his story. In fact, the other detectives on board the *Florabunda* will find out the facts, as I have anyway. And since you're not their client they will have no reason to protect you by remaining silent.'

'Then what chance do I have?'

'It's to your advantage', Pason told him, 'to have the murder solved. If the killer is found before we reach the

United States, no one will bother about you. You'd better come clean. Your information may help find the killer.'

Anderson groaned, 'All right!'

Jerry Pason and Stella Deet entered the cabin where the First Officer had assembled the other detectives – Atlas Poireau, Broderick Tourneur, Sir John Nappleby, and Mallory King.

Mr Waggish asked eagerly: 'Have you solved the murder, Mr Pason? Is that why you asked for this meeting?'

'Not yet,' Jerry Pason told him. 'But I've found out a lot about my client. Enough to clear him!'

'Did you use poetry to find out?' the First Officer asked.

'Poetry? Hell,' said the lawyer. 'None of my cases have anything to do with *literature!*

'But then, this case is different from my usual case. In my usual case, I wait till my client is on trial for murder, and till everything is going badly for him, so the prosecuting attorney is pretty sure I'm licked. Then – bang! at the last moment I find some startling new evidence, rush it into court, and save my client's life!

'But there is no court aboard ship to try Homer T. Anderson, so I will present his case to you, now.'

Jerry Pason faced the group with quiet confidence.

'The case against Homer T. Anderson', he began, 'is based chiefly on his own lies. He lied about his reasons for talking with Paul Price, about seeing Miss Price with her uncle, and about a cheque for fifteen thousand dollars. These lies were due to his fear of exposure.

'But I have discovered that he feared exposure, not for murder, but for something else! He was afraid that his business associates in New York would find out that he had tried to betray their interests when he was abroad. Price had found out about this attempt, and blackmailed him. Anderson sailed on the *Florabunda* in order to buy him off – for fifteen thousand dollars.

'That cheque is actually evidence in Anderson's favour. It means he got what he wanted from Price. He didn't need to kill him.

'And had he killed Price *after* making out the cheque he would have retrieved it at once. The fact that he waited till this morning to try to get it from Price's cabin means he did not know about the murder till the general public knew.

'If he had killed Price he would have faked an alibi. He has none.

'If he had used his own blackjack, he would not have kept it and produced it as evidence against himself.

'Someone else stole his blackjack, struck Price with it, and saved it to incriminate Anderson. Someone else found the cheque and gave it to the First Officer. Someone who wore a red and yellow scarf and had a pipe!'

'That sounds very impressive, Mr Pason,' the First Officer said in admiration. 'Can you tell us who that person is?'

'No,' the lawyer told him calmly. 'But the killer is one of the few people who saw the blackjack in the Lounge that night. He is someone who wants to endanger my client. And – according to two reliable witnesses I have just turned up – he committed the murder just before twelve-fifteen last night!

'Find that one of those people who were present when the blackjack was stolen who was on deck at twelve-fifteen, and you will have the murderer!'

CHAPTER 7

BRODERICK TOURNEUR

Quivering from stem to stern, the *Florabunda* hung poised on the crest of a heavy sea; pitched; resumed her steady rolling. The passengers in line on the boat-deck staggered. They looked self-conscious and quite amazingly clumsy in their bulky life-jackets. Like so many Tweedledums and Tweedledees armed in rubber tubings and bolsters, thought the tall man. The boat-drill, the foggy day, the murder itself, took on a new dimension of pure nonsense. He thought: Lor', what an extraordinary mess! 'A capital ship for an ocean trip was the Walloping Window-Blind.'

The *Florabunda* pitched sharply again. Farther down the line, a woman giggled. Some signal was relayed from the bridge where the Captain stood, and the drill was ended. The passengers began to disperse.

The tall man stood to let the others go by, top-heavy in their inflated rubber vests. He himself retained his customary air of aloofness, elegance, and breeding; his delicately chis-elled head emerged from his life-jacket like the head of a Velázquez nobleman from a ruff. He waited for the First Officer to catch him up. Then he said:

'You've brought me up to date on what Mr Pason, and Monsieur Poireau and Sir Jon. have done. But you haven't said what you yourself think of it all.'

Mr Waggish's agreeable, lean face became glum, and he said ruefully: 'Mr Tourneur, I'm out in the fog with no radar. No one admits taking that cosh. No one has an alibi. I've never – '

A thin, high scream was wafted up to them; it was immediately followed by shouts and staccato cries. The First Officer leapt to the rail overlooking the afterdeck and shouted down: 'What's the matter?'

A crowd of passengers was collected at the foot of the narrow companionway. Two men were helping a woman get up from the deck. Tourneur, looking down with Mr Waggish, recognized Dolores Despana. Her gleaming hair was dishevelled. Her face was white, her skirt was torn from hem to hip. She began to shake herself gingerly, and leaned over to feel her ankles.

Someone called up to Mr Waggish: 'Lady tripped and fell coming down, sir!'

'Fell!' Miss Despana repeated shrilly, straightening herself. 'Fell! I got *pushed down!*'

The First Officer seized the iron railings of the companion and swung himself down with monkeylike agility. Somewhat more cautiously, Tourneur followed him.

Miss Despana continued: 'I ought to know if I was pushed or not! It's a wonder I wasn't killed!' Her voice shook uncontrollably. She glared at the Hon. Mrs Chip-Ebberly, who was standing near-by.

Passengers who had gone on ahead came back, attracted by the clamour. On the outskirts of the crowd someone bleated: 'Murder! There's been another murder!' and there were a few more shrieks.

'*They're nervy*,' Tourneur diagnosed dispassionately.

Mrs Chip-Ebberly cleared her throat. 'I was directly behind you coming down, Miss Despana,' she observed, in a composed voice which sliced through the raw fog. She looked incredibly dowdy, respectable, and matter-of-fact. 'No one else could have pushed you. And *I* most assuredly did not do so.' She glanced downwards significantly. 'Your *fall* can be attributed to a very simple cause. If one wears such shoes on shipboard, one can only expect to trip and hurt oneself!'

Everyone stared at Dolores Despana's graceful feet. They were encased in black suede trifles, open-toed, with three-inch spiky heels – altogether as appropriate to a life-boat drill, Tourneur thought, as the silk dress the ripped skirt of which fluttered beneath her short fur jacket.

'That's it, Miss Despana,' the First Officer said in relief. 'It's those shoes. Far too pretty for climbing about a ship. And why should anyone want to push *you?*'

His gallantry did not appease her. 'Why?' Her voice was still high and uneven with shock. '*Why?* She pushed me because she wanted to kill me!' And Miss Despana's slim right index finger, marred now by a long scratch, pointed directly at Mrs Chip-Ebberly.

The older woman gave the quasi-regal toss of her head which preceded her more considered utterances. But as her eyes met Tourneur's she seemed, unaccountably, to flinch. She bit her lip. 'Really,' she said almost below her breath, 'this is quite distasteful' – and upon this genteel understatement turned and made her way through the crowd.

Hubbub broke out again and lasted until Miss Despana went off, with a large and zealous escort, to seek the Doctor – who, Tourneur suddenly realized, had not appeared at the drill. The spectators trickled away.

'Shouldn't we do something about this business?' asked Mr Waggish.

'I think,' Tourneur said, 'we might let it simmer for the nonce. Come along to Price's cabin, and I'll show you how I've been spending my time.'

Price's cabin was on the starboard side of A-deck, nearly amidships – in fact, not far from the spot on the deck outside where he had been killed and his body concealed. A portable typewriter lay open on the table, wedged securely and tied on with stout cord. The bed was turned down.

'The cabin steward says he has touched nothing since he came in last night to arrange the berth,' Tourneur said. 'His story sounded quite all right to me. Would you say he's reliable?'

Mr Waggish shook his head. 'Not my department. I expect so.'

'I'll spare you a complete inventory of Price's belongings. Everything was here – nothing in the hold; he travelled light. The luggage is frightfully dull. Wardrobe extensive but unimaginative. Hanging over there is a pretty new suit he had himself made in London – best gents' suiting, export only. Also, by the by, there's a Royal Stuart scarf with a Liberty's price tag still pinned on, and the date; that jibes with what Miss Winifred told us. Have you traced that preposterous red and yellow muffler yet? No – of course not.' Tourneur sighed. 'Well, I've managed to pick up one or two interesting items here.'

The First Officer looked up from a rather wistful inspection of the best gents' suiting, instantly alert. Gratifying, Tourneur thought. He might be my Sergeant at the yard. What would one do if there were no one to expound to? Turn schizophrenic, I dare say, and deliver lengthy lectures to one's Beta– or Watson-self. What an appalling idea! Aloud he said: 'There are no useful prints. Price's, the steward's, and some blurs. An expert might do something with them; I'm an awful duffer at it. However, look *here!*'

The ash-tray on the chest of drawers was filled with cigarette ends. Tourneur lifted one delicately with a pair of tweezers and held it up. 'These weren't here when the steward turned down the bed.'

'Lipstick marks! Why, that is a *clue!*' Mr Waggish was pleased.

Dropping the butt very carefully back into the tray, Tourneur agreed with some acerbity: 'As you say. In fact, there are *nine* little clues in the tray. It's almost too good to be true.'

'Do you mean they may have been put there to incriminate someone, Mr Tourneur – like the cosh that was thrown into Anderson's cabin?'

'Very possibly not. After all, Price did expect to meet someone here, after midnight – according to Anderson. He is not, I judge, particularly sensitive to nuances, or he might have been able to tell if Price meant a woman. But it's likely enough. If so she, at any rate, kept the appointment.'

The First Officer was discouraged. 'It could be any woman on the ship – Do we compare all their lipsticks with this colour, now?'

'Oh not quite *any* woman, I fancy,' Tourneur said rather abstractedly. Without explaining himself he continued: 'But let me show you my pet discovery – in the typewriter.' He turned the roller carefully. A fragment of paper came into sight, clinging to the platen. '*Voilà!* Now what do you deduce from that?'

'I don't know a great deal about these machines.' Mr Waggish studied it. 'I should say a sheet of paper was pulled out so roughly that it tore.'

'I should say the same. And the steward says Price sat here typing before dinner. The question is, what *became* of that paper? I've searched this room for it in vain. And it wasn't on the body.'

'Isn't it one possibility that he threw it away?'

Tourneur grimaced. 'I suppose you're right, blast you. But the steward swears there were no papers in the waste-basket. Price could have thrown it away outside the cabin, of course. But on the other hand he may have given it to someone, *Or*, you know, it may not have been he who tore it from the machine: we know someone else was in here, from the lipstick marks, and the fact that the cheque was taken away.'

Mr Waggish touched a leather briefcase. 'You haven't said anything about this, Mr Tourneur.'

Tourneur groaned. 'Because I can hardly bear to think of the damn thing. It contains clippings from that newspaper column of Price's. To that loathsome series of compositions have I devoted untold hours of perfectly good sea voyage.'

Mr Waggish said apologeticaly, 'I'm afraid this is no holiday for you.'

'My dear man, it's not your fault.' Tourneur looked at the briefcase with extreme distaste. 'I should not like to figure in that column for praise or blame. Which is preferable, would you say – to be exposed for peculation, or publicly congratulated on divorcing one's fifth wife? On my word, I think our murderer showed good taste.'

'Are there any items about people aboard ship?'

Tourneur screwed his face up. 'You do keep a fellow on his toes,' he observed mildly. 'No. Of course, I've not had time to check the whole passenger list; but none of the people we're interested in seems to figure. *However*, I found a few clippings from magazines and newspapers which I take to be raw material for future Price lucubrations. This batch, for instance – reviews of a play. Notice the bits he underlined in red pencil!'

'Miss Dolores Despana, the supporting player in this offensive jumble of diluted Coward, resuscitated Barrie, and unidentifiable bawdy, with a touching fidelity to the author's spirit, made not the faintest discernible endeavour to infuse the breath of life into a wooden role. Her performance is comprehensible, indeed, only if one assumes that she mistook

83

the boards of the Old Empire for the stage of a mannequin parade. How long must we tolerate the vulgar and insipid . . .'

'The other reviews', said Tourneur, 'are rather less turgid, but equally emphatic. Miss Despana was not a critical success.'

'Poor lass,' the First Officer said unexpectedly. 'Do you mean to say that that blighter was going to quote these reviews in his column, back in the States?' His blue eyes shone indignantly; he threw the papers down and examined another clipping. 'What's this?'

Tourneur said. 'That's what I should like to know, Mr Waggish.'

The clipping was a photograph in sepia, on glossy paper. It depicted a row of dullish-looking middle-aged persons, all looking genteelly unaware of the neighbourhood of camera. The label read: 'The Bishop's Baxton Bazaar; Lord Stone, Colonel Putter, Mrs Putter, Mrs Fitzhug Moppet, Lady Stone, and the Hon. Mrs Chip-Ebberly.'

'I should like to know,' Tourneur repeated. 'Maybe Miss Price can tell us; I'll stop by and ask her. Meanwhile, perhaps you'd be good enough to have someone track down Miss Despana and ask her if we may have a little talk with her.'

'In her cabin?'

'No,' said Tourneur. 'I rather think, in here.'

Winifred Price disclaimed all knowledge of her uncle's column. He used to type the copy himself, from rough notes, she said; but she had never looked at them. 'I never even read it when it was printed', she insisted, fixing her pretty dark eyes on Tourneur with immense seriousness. 'It was just a sadistic, *anti-social* piece of exhibitionism. I wouldn't have a thing to do with it!' As Tourneur eyed her gravely, she flushed. 'That's pretty vile, isn't it!' she said with a sort of melancholy, masochistic pride. 'His writing supported me, and I suppose I'm inheriting the profits, and I look down my nose at it. But it isn't snobbery, *honestly!*'

Tourneur said gently: 'I didn't suppose it was.'

'But it's – priggish!' She blushed again. 'You think I'm a prig. And a *hypocrite!*' Tears came to her eyes.

'Oh, my dear child!' Tourneur protested, his left eyebrow climbing high into his forehead and his mouth stretching to one side. 'Don't torment yourself. Please!' He held out a clean handkerchief with a winning smile. 'Do try to help me, instead. I should like most awfully to know anything you can tell me about these clippings.'

Winifred sniffed, wiped her eyes, and sat up straight. At the picture he extended to her, she cried: 'Why – that's Mrs Chip-Ebberly!'

'It is indeed. Did your uncle know her?'

The girl knit her brow thoughtfully. 'I don't think he ever mentioned her name. But I do remember this picture, though her name and her face meant nothing to me when I saw it before. Uncle Paul tore it out of some magazine. I saw him trimming the edges with his scissors.'

Tourneur asked very quietly: 'Was that on the same day, Miss Price, that he told you that you would be sailing on the *Florabunda?*'

'I – Why, yes, it was.' She opened her eyes very wide. 'How in the world did you now?'

Tourneur smiled. He said lightly: 'You must allow me a few poor mysteries. If I gave my secret away you'd see what a slow-witted chap I really am.'

Winifred Price gazed up at him and blushed a third time. 'Oh,' she said fervently. 'Oh, Mr Tourneur; no one would *ever* think *that!*'

Dolores Despana bestowed a brilliant smile on Tourenur and the First Officer, and sank on to a chair with languid grace. The damages resulting from her fall had been repaired. She wore a black silk jersey frock, cut very low, with a sparkling clip. She looked expensive, dashing, over-made up, and extremely lovely.

An expert little piece of goods, Tourneur thought as he lit her cigarette with his unfailing courtesy. Aloud he said: 'Thank you for coming, Miss Despana; we – '

'That's O.K.,' she interrupted. 'It's a pleasure to meet you. When they said your name first, I thought you were just a Mr *Turner*. I didn't know it was spelled T-o-u-r-n-e-u-r! Why, I used to see your picture in the papers in London, "Handsome Tourneur", only I didn't know how to pronounce it. I thought you were just terribly good-looking – '

Tourneur said remotely: 'You are very kind. I – '

'Anyway, I love an English accent. You're what they call a bobby, aren't you?'

Mr Waggish was scandalized. 'Mr Tourneur is a gentleman,' he said, with an apologetic glance at Tourneur's superlative tailoring. '*Everyone* knows that! Why, he went to Oxf – '

Tourneur lifted a thin hand in deprecation. 'If you'd be so good as to help us, Miss Despana,' he said formally. 'You have been asked already, I believe, if you know who took Mr Anderson's cosh – '

'I've been thinking,' said Dolores Despana. 'And now I know who took it. That old biddy. The Hon-or-a-bul Mrs Something Ebberly.'

The coarse mockery grated on Tourneue: nothing else in her composition, he thought, quite matched the miraculous finish of her complexion. But he sensed something deep underneath the vulgarity. She is afraid, he told himself. She is truly, pitifully afraid. He asked slowly: 'You saw Mrs Chip-Ebberly take it?'

'No, but she thinks I saw her. I know, because she tried to kill me after the boat-drill.'

Tourneur frowned. 'You have made that accusation before, I think, Miss Despana. How do you *know* that Mrs Chip-Ebberly tried to kill you?'

'How?' Miss Despana replied simply: 'Because she thought I'd seen her take the blackjack.'

Tourneur was momentarily bereft of speech by this maddening convolution of logic. Then he asked patiently: 'Have you any notion *why* she should have taken it, Miss Despana – that is, why she should have wished to kill Price?'

The actress said readily: 'He had something on her, of course.'

Tourneur shifted ground abruptly. 'How long had you known Mr Price, please?'

She drew on her cigarette before replying. 'Well,' she said at last, with an effect of preternatural frankness, 'I was doing a show in London. *Hot Legs*. He saw it, so he wanted to meet me. He sent flowers, and so on. . . . Then when he found I was sailing home on the same ship he – well you know how it is. He *pursued* me.' She looked from Tourneur to the First

Officer with a slow, practised smile which would have been
called a simper on a plainer woman, but which quite dissolved
Mr Waggish's critical faculties. He nodded in complete
conviction.

Tourneur wondered: 'And can she really expect me to
accept this picture of that cynical and scabrous journalist as
– an infatuated stage-door Johnny? How exceedingly stupid
she must be – or exceedingly sure of herself!' He fixed his
eyes on a point just over Miss Despana's head and murmured:
'Quite.'

'So finally, last night, he offered to give me a plug in his
column. So he wrote that piece about how I was a great
sensation abroad.'

Tourneur felt himself go suddenly taut. When he spoke his
voice was expressionless. 'Ah, yes. You say he offered to
write this – "plug" last night?'

'Just before dinner. We were having cocktails. That was
the last time I ever saw him.'

Tourneur looked at her thoughtfully again. He said: 'We
are trying to identify a woman who came to this cabin last
night.' As this venture elicited only a stare of babylike glassi-
ness which achieved the suggestion of an incredible innocence
not merely of this particular rendezvous but of unconven-
tional behaviour in general, he went on. 'She left certain
traces of her presence behind.' With a swift, delicate gesture
he produced the ash-tray, which had been hidden by his chair.
'She wore a Corono lipstick; the shade, I think,' he said
diffidently, 'is "Scarlet Ecstasy".'

Dolores Despana's aggressive ignorance was unshaken. 'I
can't imagine who it would be,' she returned, looking calmly
at the little heap of stained cigarette ends.

'I see. Thank-you. . . . Now, Miss Despana,' Tourneur
went on cheerfully, 'about this "plug" which Mr Price promised to write for you: do you think he meant to keep his
promise?'

'I – It was more than a *promise*.' Her eyes narrowed a
little. 'What are you getting at? You know perfectly well that
he wrote it!'

Tourneur asked quietly: 'How *should* I know, Miss
Despana?'

'Because – ' Miss Despana's eyes jerked wide open. A look

at once of fury and of terror crossed her face; it was as if she had just sighted a peculiarly diabolical trap. She jumped to her feet. 'You *won't* get me mixed up in this!' she cried harshly, and flung herself out of the room.

And it was typical of the drunken perversity of the whole case, Tourneur thought, that she should have shot out into the passageway at the precise moment when Mrs Chip-Ebberly was passing the door, with a resulting collision which would, he thought, no doubt have been a wild hit at the Palladium.

Mrs Chip-Ebberly clutched at the doorpost to keep from falling as Miss Despana flounced away. She refused the seat Tourneur offered her.

'Perhaps since you are here,' he said, 'you will have the great kindness to give us one moment of your time . . . You have stated, I believe, that you did not know Mr Price. Had you any reason to suppose that he was seeking your acquaintance? For there is some evidence that he was interested in you.'

'Fantastic!' The tone conveyed only affront as at an impropriety, and her face was guarded; but Tourneur saw her hands close convulsively on the wooden handles of her knitting-bag. She looked at the clipping Tourneur produced. A curious expression flickered across her rigid features, and when she spoke her relief was unmistakable. 'I cannot imagine,' she said, 'why he should have had this in his possession.'

'Thank you very much. And you have, I suppose, no suggestions as to who might have killed Mr Price?'

'None', Mrs Chip-Ebberly replied pointedly, 'other than those I have already transmitted to the authorities.' She explained with a glance of majestic rebuke in the direction of Mr Waggish, who ran his finger under his collar in agitation: 'As I have informed the First Officer and Sir Jon. Nappleby, Mr Price consorted with two individuals of the type who invariably figure in crimes: Mr Anderson and a — a woman passenger.' On these last words, she glanced about the cabin with a grimness which made the two investigators suddenly conscious of a heavy scent clinging to the very bulkheads, of thick cigarette smoke and a general aura of some orgy just ended.

'Lumme!' Mr Waggish ejaculated when she had left.

'Lumme, indeed.'

After a moment the First Officer said rather unhappily: 'You think Miss Despana did it, don't you, Mr Tourneur?'

'Oh, my dear chap, I don't especially think she killed Price! But she came here to meet him, unquestionably. And I think she will be back, and anxious to convince us that she *was* here. But I fancy she'll wait till she can handle one of us alone.'

'Oh.' Mr Waggish digested this prophecy solemnly. 'I hadn't known', he said presently, 'that a detective had so many – so many . . .'He waved his hand inarticulately.

'Emotional crises?' Tourneur sighed. 'I've known cases where those two ladies, and the rather theatrical little Miss Price, would appear as nothing. One does need to be able to cope with them.'

'Is that the most important qualification for being a detective, would you say, Mr Tourneur?'

Tourneur reflected. 'That, and breeding. One always has to ask oneself, "How does the gentleman behave in this particular situation?" Or – better still – "How would a lady consider that a gentleman ought to behave in this particular situation?" ' And no handbooks, no rules, no police colleges can teach such things, he thought. He accepted thankfully Mr Waggish's subsequent invitation to have a quick one before dinner in the Doctor's cabin.

They found the Doctor and the Purser comfortably ensconced among the former's cluttered possessions. The Doctor jumped up to fetch more glasses from a cabinet under his bunk. 'Well, have you solved the crime yet, Mr Tourneur?' he asked in his homely Newcastle voice. 'Cheers!'

Mr Waggish intervened. 'Let Mr Tourneur have a drink in peace. This voyage is a busman's holiday for him. . . . Cheers!'

Tourneur smiled. 'I like to think out loud when I can corner an audience. Perhaps you'll let me run through things.' He settled back in his chair. 'Apparently only a few persons had the opportunity to obtain the weapon which killed Price: I hear you've definitely decided it was the cosh that did it, Doctor? Well, did these persons all have the opportunity to kill him at twelve-fifteen? And did they all have motive? First off, we'll leave Mr Mallory King, who noticed the theft, out of consideration.'

'Well,' Mr Waggish said, 'practically anyone on the ship had the opportunity to commit murder, at twelve-fifteen or any time whatever. No one seems to have an alibi, and it's not to be expected they should, at night, with no regular habits, among strangers, and all.'

'Too true.' Tourneur sighed. 'Oh, for a village, where everyone knows where his neighbours belong at a given time! Well, as to motives, then. Miss Price gains financially by her uncle's death, and she had various complicated reasons for resenting him. Anderson was being blackmailed by him, but how did he get his cosh back? And Miss Despana and Mrs Chip-Ebberly had some connexion with him also. We don't know yet if they had reason to wish him dead.'

The Purser asked quickly: 'You say Mrs Chip-Ebberly — What could she have to do with a bloke like him?'

'I don't know. But I rather think', Tourneur said, 'that Mr Price sailed on this ship because he learned she would be aboard.'

'Not his type, I should have thought,' the Doctor muttered irreverently.

Tourneur explained sedately: 'Price cut the good lady's picture out of a magazine on the very day he told his niece they had passage on the *Florabunda*. Now, Miss Price told Monsieur Poireau that her uncle made that announcement directly after telling her that he had come upon "two nice pieces of business;" he was pleased about some "tittle-tattle". "Someone had tattled." I *think* those were the words she quoted; I have a filthy memory,' Tourneur interposed apologetically, Mr Waggish looked at him, opened his mouth to speak, but closed it again. Tourneur continued: 'Now just look at this picture of Mrs Chip-Ebberly and her rather forbidding friends at the Bazaar. Miss Price is American and doesn't know our society papers; but *we* can tell that this picture is from the *Tatler!* From which one deduces that it was this picture in the *Tatler* which had something to do with Price's taking passage on this ship.'

'So that he could meet Mrs Chip-Ebberly, do you mean? I can't believe he could have anything on *her!*' the Purser insisted.

'Too much the perfect comic dowager, you think? Maybe. On the other hand, there's that grotesque business of her stalking Anderson like a self-appointed and miscast Mata Hari. It's so damn ridiculous it just might be a giant smoke screen.'

The Doctor reached over to refill Tourneur's glass. He asked: 'And that's the whole list; and no one has an alibi?'

Tourneur studied him and the other two officers for a moment. He asked himself if they could really be so naïve as they appeared. 'That exhausts the *passengers* who are suspect.' He underlined the noun. 'If you'll forgive me for being tiresome,' he went on diffidently, 'I might make a note of your alibis. Just for the record – since you were all on the scene when that bothersome cosh was taken.'

The Doctor looked blank; the Purser, uncomfortable; and the First Officer, at first surprised and then decidedly chagrined.

'But if I'd seen who took it,' he pointed out reasonably, 'I'd have said. So would these chaps. You didn't see who took it, did you?' he asked them.

The Doctor shook his head, but the Purser said dryly, 'Inspector Tourneur wants a bit more than that.' He eyed Tourneur curiously, almost resentfully, and Tourneur was faintly puzzled. The Purser, even if he was younger, struck him as more a man of the world than the other officers – though they all appeared, each with a certain amount of charm, to be fundamentally and almost fecklessly impractical. He said lightly:

'Well, if this were a book, you know, I should be obliged to give a portentous frown, take out my notebook, and ask you each: "Where were you at quarter after midnight on the night of the murder?"'

'*We* were up on the boat-deck then, Waggish,' said the Doctor. Turning to Tourneur he explained complacently: 'The First was listening to "Tipptoppus and Gazella".'

Mr Waggish hesitated. 'Was it so early?'

'Don't you remember,' the Doctor said, 'you came up at seven bells, and when the steward brought us that cocoa he said it was still just on five minutes of the hour?'

'Aye, you're right.'

91

'And you were together every minute,' Tourneur asked, 'from eleven-thirty (wouldn't that be?) until – '

'Every minute till nearly six bells,' said the Doctor. 'I got through three cantos.'

Mr Waggish answered Tourneur's interrogatory glance with a nod. He was a little grim at the recollection of three solid hours of 'Tipptoppus and Gazella', and Tourneur who had heard about the Doctor's epic, felt sympathetic; the more so as the Doctor now began to declaim:

'At midnight dim and dire Sarazin called all his hosts –
Chimaeras, elves, and demons, goblins, incubi, and ghosts,
Werewolves and vampires, witches foul that sail upon the wind,
Dread wizards, sorcerers, necromancers, scourges of mankind . . .'

Tourneur was reminded of the Dormouse at the Mad Tea Party who fell asleep singing 'Twinkle twinkle twinkle twinkle . . .' The Doctor's friends did not silence him with pinches, or by thrusting his head into a teapot, but they seemed able by dint of long practice to ignore him.

'And you, Tom?' Mr Waggish demanded over the incantation. 'After you'd left your girl and gone below, that is?'

The Purser said stiffly: 'I wasn't alone for a minute! We played cards in the Engineers' Mess – the Chief, Sparks, the Fourth, and myself. You'll find they confirm my alibi! We were there for hours.'

'Nor was the noble Tippitop from their dread power secure,
Nor by his shield of adamant, nor by his bosom pure – '

'Anyway,' the Purser went on in a loud tense voice, 'even if I couldn't account for every minute – which I can! – *why should I have killed Price!*'

'We know you didn't do it, you clot,' the First Officer said. He added heartlessly: 'But I'll lay Mr Tourneur could make a case against you if he wished.'

'Well,' Tourneur said apologetically, 'in a book the detective would say. First, this chap's alibi is too perfect. What innocent man would have every second covered by a shoal of witnesses? And then he'd say: This chap didn't like Price. Price insulted him in a rather public place. If the insult were unjustified, *there's* a motive. Or, supposing it was a true accusation, and this chap did hope to marry the wealthy niece, her fiancé being at a considerable remove – '

The Purser's ruddy face darkened as Tourneur elaborated this hypothesis. Now he cried: 'That's an insult to Miss Price!' Without another word he rose and hurled himself incontinently at Tourneur.

'Belay there!' Mr Waggish grabbed his arm, shocked.

The Doctor looked on with lively but seemingly Olympian interest; his only concession to the emergency was to move a glass out of the way of harm from the Purser's flailing arms. Tourneur had not risen from his chair. One eyebrow lifted high, he studied the Purser's indignant face. I have evidently overestimated his sophistication, he thought. It's as choleric a young fellow as ever was. . . . And he wondered just what he ought to read into that.

The spasm of fury ended as abruptly as it had begun. The Purser sat down, picked up his glass, and said: 'Sorry, Mr Tourneur. I know you didn't really mean . . . I'm afraid I lost my temper.' He sounded genuinely matter-of-fact and even a little pleased. Rather obstinately he added: 'But my alibi will hold, you know. Price was a blasted rat; he mistreated – *her*. But *I* was playing cards when he got killed; and I have no idea who did it!'

Tourneur found a visitor waiting in his cabin. Dolores Despana had changed her style from the chic to the delicate. She wore a coral lipstick, a pale green chiffon gown, and the air of a woman frail, defenceless, but brave. Very possibly she could not act, he thought; but she could at least *look* the part of a heroine from Pinero or Henry Arthur Jones. She carried a tiny, glittering evening bag and a lacy handkerchief, which she occasionally remembered to touch to her eyes. She began in a faltering voice, one hand laid confidingly on Tourneur's, 'I should have known better than to fib to a *famous detective like you!*'

'Thank you very much,' he said formally.

'But the way it must *look!* Being in that cabin so *late at night!*'

Tourneur could think of no really civil answer to this; he made an encouraging noise.

'Not that there was anything *wrong!* Like I told you, Paul promised to write a plug for me, only he said I'd have to come to his stateroom for a conference about it. So, of course I thought twelve-thirty was pretty late; but it couldn't hurt to go. So I knocked and went in and waited for a while, and when he didn't show up after five minutes I went away.'

'After smoking', Tourneur murmured vaguely, 'nine cigarettes.'

'I – yes,' she said rather flatly. She put the handkerchief to one eye and then, after consideration, to the other.

'So that it was, perhaps, rather more than five minutes?'

'I – Oh, hell,' said Miss Despana in a welcome burst of candour. 'He was a rat. But a plug from him means – It was a case of my *career!* And besides, if I'd refused to go – ' She stopped.

'Yes, Miss Despana?'

'Nothing.'

'Perhaps I know already,' he said, not unkindly. 'Price was not a generous man. He may have threatened to print excerpts from the London reviews – '

She cried: 'They had a grudge against the director! It was all dirty politics. Why, the – '

'Yes. Well,' Tourneur said cheerfully, 'since we've got over all that, suppose you tell me what happened in Price's cabin as you waited?'

'Happened? Why, nothing happened,' said Dolores Despana with devastating *gaucherie*. 'He got killed, didn't he? He never came.'

'Quite so,' Tourneur said hastily. 'I meant to inquire as to anything – er – *else* that may have taken place. Did you notice anything remarkable about the cabin?' At her blank stare, he experienced a spasm of irritation: her slowness of mind appeared to be genuine. He suggested: 'Was there anything on the floor?'

'Oh. That's right. There was an envelope.'

Tourneur nodded: that would be Anderson's cheque. He asked slowly: 'Did anyone knock, or try to enter?'

'No. Nothing happened, only I got sleepy waiting. I was mad, too, naturally,' she added in another disconcerting flare of frankness, 'but next morning when I heard he'd been killed I knew why he hadn't showed up, so *that* was O.K.'

Tourneur looked at her speculatively as she produced this sufficiently inhuman sentiment. He asked: 'Do you mind telling me just what Mr Price said in his "plug"?'

'Why, it says how I set London on fire, how I was seen with a lord, and – But *you* know! It was right there in his typewriter. That's how you got me to admit I was in the cabin, isn't it? Why ask me to tell you what it said?' She gasped in sudden alarm. 'There isn't going to be any hold-up about getting it printed, is there? I mean, they'll put his column in the papers even if he's dead, won't they? *Sure* they will! I know they do; they publish things post – post – '

Tourneur suddenly felt like a brute. 'Miss Despana,' he said slowly. 'I don't know about posthumous publication in this case. I did use that typed paper with the "plug" as a subterfuge, I'm afraid; you must forgive me. I *guessed* it was in the typewriter. I have never seen it.'

Dolores Despana stood up abruptly. She cried with an appalling effect of shrewishness: 'What are you getting at? What do you mean, you didn't see it? It was right there! Have you burned it up or something?'

Tourneur sighed. 'Miss Despana, I give you my word I'd like to see it almost as much as you would. But when I got to Price's cabin there was nothing left in the machine but a scrap of paper. Someone went into the cabin after you had left and tore that paper out.'

'She told the truth about seeing the paper in the typewriter,' Tourneur said to the First Officer. 'Of course she *might* have killed him and then pretended to wait for him, leaving ostentatious clues, so we'd think she didn't know he was dead. But someone else took her precious plug – and the envelope with the cheque. And who would do that but the murderer? . . . Which takes us around in a circle.'

'Do you have any theory who it is, Mr Tourneur?'

Tourneur grimaced. 'Have you ever played Horribles?' As the First Office shook his head uncomprehendingly, he explained: 'They do it at parties. You draw a head and fold the paper over. The next person draws the shoulders and the arms and the body to the waist; and the next one goes on down to the knees; and so on. They you unfold the paper, and there is a figure with a girl's head and a gorilla's chest and a ballet skirt and the legs of a duck. Everyone roars with laughter.'

Mr Waggish looked at him in solemn question.

'I feel', Tourneur explained, 'as if we were all hard at play at Horribles. Monsieur Poireau draws a head, and Nappleby a chest, and so on. What sort of monster will this murderer turn out to be? We're working almost blindfold.'

The First Office stammered a little in his distress. 'I've tried to tell each of you what the others are doing, how the investigation is going on. I know I'm not much of a chap for talking, but – '

'My dear chap!' Tourneur was appalled. Damn, he thought; now I've hurt his feelings! Aloud he said very charmingly: 'You've done splendidly! You are the perfect liaison agent, Watson, and *raisonneur!*' And, as Mr Waggish became quite crimson with suppressed pleasure, he went on cheerfully: 'And we've found out a bit about the fair Dolores. And we know someone was in that cabin. We know there's something to be found out about Mrs Chip-Ebberly. We *are* a bit forrader, after all!'

CHAPTER 8

TRAJAN BEARE

(From the notebook of Ernie Woodbin)

Beare was sitting up in bed, in his pyjamas, the way he had been all his waking hours, and he was drinking beef-tea.

I reported: 'Latitude and longitude about the same, heavy following sea, still foggy, average speed fifteen knots. There's a movie in the dining-saloon at eight-thirty, but I've already seen it. Paul Price was murdered last night.'

I watched his face for a reaction but wasn't surprised to see none. He just took another sip of beef-tea. I went on with the daily bulletin:

'They don't know yet who did it. But of course when they come to question me, and they find out you told me to keep Price out of your way by force if necessary – '

'Ernie. I have asked you before. Please don't play the clown till we reach shore.'

'Yes, sir. It may cramp my style in the investigation, having to play it straight.'

He looked at me then.

I nodded. 'No kidding. His head was bashed in.'

Beare let out a sigh. 'So. I cannot pretend any regret. Price was unprincipled, illiterate, and a boor. The Press and the nation are to be congratulated.'

'That's what the Captain thinks too. When he heard about it he said, "Good." He seemed to think that ended the matter. But there are five detectives hot on the trail already – '

Beare interrupted. 'The salmon last night was respectable. For lunch I will have it again. A clear soup . . .'

This meant the matter was ended as far as he was

concerned too, and that I was to shut up. He spent the next four minutes talking, not too nostalgically, about food. I stood it as long as I could, and then wandered off.

The next few hours I just moseyed about, keeping an eye on the trend of events. It isn't often that you get a chance to watch your top professional rivals at work, close at hand, and I had to admit some of their techniques looked good, like Poireau twirling that moustache and Nappleby spouting polysyllables and Brody Tourneur always behaving as if he was at a garden pary; but after careful study and comparison I decided I'd stick to my own methods, and I still liked Beare's way of using his eyes, and pursing his lips.

Beare never said a word about the murder, and I refrained from heckling him. But I had a feeling it wouldn't stay so simple as that, and I was right. Not counting the general request for help they'd issued when Price's body was discovered and the Purser pointed out that there were professional man-hunters on board the *Florabunda*, we had three special invitations to join the fun.

Late the next afternoon the First Officer came up and we fell to talking. He was about my age, tall for a Limey, with blue eyes and a swell tan, and I'd got the impression that, while his brains might never set the Atlantic ablaze, he was good company and nice to have on a ship where the Captain was balmy and might decide on an all-out effort to break the Atlantic speed record any moment. I asked him if he'd caught the killer yet and he said no, quite seriously.

'Mr Beare is a great detective, isn't he?' he asked. 'One of the best?'

'*The* best, I'd say,' I told him. 'And he'd agree. He's a genius. Why?'

'Well, you don't suppose – '

'If you're hinting he might like to play cops and robbers too, it's no use. He only plays for million-dollar bills.'

'Oh, I see. Well, I didn't really hope he would. I mean, I've heard he's hard to persuade.'

'When there isn't a fee, he's reinforced concrete,' I said. 'Anyway, this time I don't see why you want him. You've got enough guys at work.'

'It's only that there isn't much time, and I thought the more investigators we had – '

'Uh-uh,' I told him. 'It's the law of diminishing returns. Could you sail the ship better if you had nine captains?'

'I see what you mean, Mr Woodbin,' he said. He let out a yawn. 'It's bad enough *one* Old Man . . . I could do with some sleep. And a drink.'

So we had a drink, and then another. I told him about working for Beare, and about Ohio, where I grew up and which he thought was part of southern California. I set him straight on that, and he told me about the *Florabunda*. He said life at sea wasn't fit for a human being, and after just one or two more trips he was going to quit and retire to a tropical island he knew about where he could live like a king for ten bob a year. Since at the current exchange that meant about twelve cents a month and no income tax, I figured he had a good thing there, but I took him with a grain of salt. I'd heard sailors talk like that before, and in my experience they never quit till they can't totter across a gang-plank any longer.

That was the first request for help, and I didn't even bother passing it on to Beare. The second one he knew about for the simple reason that it was delivered to him in person. I was with him when there was a knock at the door, and thinking it was the steward with his beer I yelled, 'Come in.' It was Dolores Despana. She walked right in while I was off my guard.

Beare glared. He may have recognized her from things I'd said, or he may not. It didn't matter. What with his general feeling about women, which is not favourable, and his being away from solid ground, I half expected him to say outright to get out; but he only looked at me in a way that meant I was to say it.

But I ignored him and looked at Dolores. You could tell that two years ago she'd been buying clothes on Fourteenth Street, and that one year ago she kept a wad of chewing-gum in her cheek; but she was coming along fast and there was certainly nothing wrong with what the eye could see. I said, 'This is Miss Despana,' and got her settled in a chair.

Beare inclined his head about one-eighth of an inch and continued to glare. Dolores stared at him and asked, 'You're Trajan Beare?' He didn't reply, and she answered herself, 'Yeah,' in a soft voice as if she'd heard but hadn't ever quite believed a man could be that fat. Once she'd got it established that it was possible, she lost interest, and said in a very businesslike way:

'You take clients, don't you? I want you to do a job for me.'

Beare gave no sign that he heard. I said, 'Sorry, Mr Beare isn't taking – '

But she went right on: 'You find out who killed people. I've seen about you in the papers. Well, I don't care about that, I didn't kill Paul Price, I certainly don't care who did. But he wrote a plug for me and someone stole it.'

'You want Mr Beare to find it?' I asked her.

She shook her head. 'No, Anyone who's enough of a stinker to steal it and keep it from me would be stinker enough to burn it up, or throw it overboard,' She looked ready to cry. 'It would have put me into the big time on Broadway, that plug!'

Beare spoke at last, frowning, 'I don't follow you, madam. You do not fear being arrested for the murder yourself. You do not wish to have the murderer caught. You consider search for this document useless. Why do you want to hire me?'

She eyed him as if he wasn't so bright as she'd heard. '*Publicity*' she said impatiently. 'What do you *think*? You're a name. If you work on this case as my agent, we'll both get a good Press! You can do it on a percentage basis, a percentage of the profits on my next show. It might be almost as good as a plug in Price's column.'

At that point I cut in. Beare looked like exploding, and I felt almost the same. Her thinking Beare, who charged fees that turned strong bank presidents pale, would do anything contingent on the success of a non-existent Broadway show, was bad enough. But letting him know she was willing to use him as a second-best for Paul Price, who was illiterate, unprincipled, and a boor – I took her elbow firmly and got the door open.

'Sorry,' I said. 'Mr Beare would love to help, but he's suffering from *mal de mer*, that's Portuguese for sea-sickness, and he might do you more harm than good.' I got her into the passageway and let her go. 'One last word,' I said as she flounced. 'Just some brotherly advice. Try Anderson. He may not be pretty; but he's rich, and he's lonesome. Nobody on board likes him very much.' I gave her a big smile and went up on deck for air. I didn't want to discuss the thing with Beare. I knew what he'd say, and anyway I hadn't made up my mind about Dolores. She could be what she looked like, a gorgeous dumb blonde on the make, but I'd been fooled before, often enough to think twice before deciding.

That was the second invitation. The third was anonymous and informal; in fact it was an invitation only if you read between the lines.

I found it on the floor of my stateroom, in a *Florabunda* envelope that was gummed shut. Thinking it was a notice, I let it ride until morning, and I could have kicked myself when I slit it open and pulled out a sheet of business paper, typed double-space over all of one side, with a rough torn bottom edge.

I'd followed things closely enough so I knew what it was all right, and even though it wasn't technically any business of mine I got that feeling you get when something breaks in a case. I sat down and began to read it. The first paragraph was the plug for Dolores Despana and was just another plug if you didn't know the story behind it.

'The de-luscious Dolores Despana has waved byebye to Johnny Bull after setting London on fire with the biggest blaze since ye olde incendiary bombs. . . . Her *Hot Legs* had them drooling. . . . Saw her wining in Leicester Square with a certain Marquis of you know where, and it's not too far from those white cliffs. But Dolores tells me she's true to Times Square. And yours truly predicts Times Square will be hearing a lot about this gal!'

Then there was a piece of Hollywood dirt, standard Price stuff:

'Jackie O'Dair insists it's still rings on the finger and bells in the steeple for her and Tony. Says Tony is in Mexico vacationing. But yours truly saw Tony with "friend" Mae in Paris, and it looks like Lohengrin for him and her. Maybe Tony's *en route* to Mexico via the Champs-Elysées. How about that, Jackie?'

And then the pay-off:

'Told you about the so-called brains we have on this barge. Well I find there is another master-mind on board who is a horse of a different colour. He is a specialist in murder too but from another angle and he is having fun and games whilst the Sherlocks sleep. He does not know I have found him out but next time we meet FIREWORKS MAY BE EXPECTED. THE REAL NAME OF THIS CROOK IS NOT ON HIS PASSPORT IT IS GIB.'

It ended there. By that time I was goggle-eyed. This murder had been screwy enough before; now it was for Krafft-Ebing's casebook. I got up and carried the goddam thing to Beare's cabin, holding it by the edges just as a matter of principle. I was pretty sure there wouldn't be any prints.

Beare was ordering breakfast. He nodded politely and said, 'Good morning, Ernie.'

When the steward had gone I told him what I had.

Beare shrugged and picked up the book he was reading.

'You don't think it's a clue?'

'No'.

'You think it's a frame?'

'No.' Beare turned a page.

'Then – Okay. I get it, You're not interested.'

'Ernie.' Beare put his book down on his belly. 'Ernie. I am aware that ever since this murder was discovered you have tried to needle me into undertaking its investigation.'

'I thought it might occupy your mind,' I said earnestly. 'The good secretary always tries to – '

'Pfui. Even if we were at home instead of – ' Beare closed his eyes and came to a full stop. It was practically the only time I've ever heard him leave a sentence unfinished. He opened his eyes and said patiently: 'Even if we were at home, I should not take the case. Why should I? There is no client, no fee. Public spirit? I do not condone the murder even of a scurrilous quidnunc, but its investigation does not devolve on me; there are representatives of the constituted authorities aboard who have it in hand. This paper should be taken to the official in charge, at once.'

'Just say you're too lazy – '

'Enough, Ernie. I do not know the facts, but, viewing the case cursorily, I doubt if it is soluble. A dolt could get away with a crime, under such circumstances. The obstacles in the way of detecting him are insuperable. We cannot trace the past histories of scores of passengers. We cannot distinguish between their normal behaviour and their abnormal deviations. We cannot check alibis. The murderer may be some Ordinary Seaman with a grudge against passengers. He may be a rival journalist, incognito. He may be the Captain.'

Making a speech meant Beare was more at ease, anyway. I said, just to keep things going: 'You're the boss. And if one of the other detectives solves the case – well, you're still the *fattest* one, they can't take that away from you.'

Beare growled. 'Least of all will you move me by appeals to my spirit of emulation. My taste runs neither to socialized detection nor' – he grimaced – 'to relay races.' He picked up his book, and I beat it, carrying the paper.

In my cabin I looked at it again. I hated to let it go just like that, and I played around with the idea of a little investigating on my own; but in the end I decided to take it to the First Officer. After all, we had been palsy over gin and orange, and he had confided in me his plans for the future, so I ought to play fair. When I finally tracked him down and showed him the paper he got as excited as if it was going to have the murderer's signature on it. But when he'd read it through he said:

'I can't understand this. It's daft! There's something strange about it. . . . Has Mr Beare seen it? What does he think?'

'He won't touch it.'

'What the devil does it mean? Do you think that Price had discovered that he was going to be killed?'

'It sounds that way. I wish he had had time to go on, or more space – it breaks off short.'

'Do you think he was going to give the actual *name?* But what begins with G-i-b?'

'My guess is he was going to say "gibberish",' I told him. 'But I've got other questions. Who took the paper out of the machine, and why was it put in my cabin?'

Mr Waggish gave a groan. 'Maybe there's *a third* person at work, do you suppose? It's daft. Completely daft!'

'Cheer up,' I said.

'Oh,' he said, 'I don't care, personally. In fact I'm rather enjoying the experience, it's different from the usual crossing. But the Old Man – he's already all fouled up like Christ in a whirlpool. And if we have to wait in quarantine on account of this – '

'In quarantine?'

103

'If we don't have the criminal, we shall have to wait offshore. And then the Skipper will really blow up, and we'll have the hell of a trip back home. He hates every day we spend in sight of land.'

I could have told him that was nothing to what Beare felt about every day in sight of open ocean, but I let it go. I said 'So long' and went to Beare's cabin again. I'd decided the time had come for some more needling, this time a good jab, hypodermic size.

Beare was sitting up reading. He put the book down and said: 'Three more nights, and we will dine at home. I shall radiogram ahead about the menu. There will be *saucisse minuit –* '

'It *would* be nice,' I said wistfully.

Beare blinked, and I guessed he was looking at me suspiciously as I turned my back and went to the porthole to look at the fog. I gave him the latest weather report, and began a blow-by-blow description of the movie I hadn't gone to in the dining-saloon.

'Ernie. What the devil are you insinuating?'

I said cheerily: 'Nothing, probably. With all these great Sherlocks on board the crime ought to be solved before too long. Chances are we won't be delayed more than one or two nights.'

'Ernie!'

I explained what the First Officer had told me.

Beare's chin quivered. 'Confound it!' He drew a deep breath. 'Confound it! Very well. Tell me what has been done so far.'

So that was how we got into the case. Beare sat there scowling while I went over it in detail, not leaving anything out, even the flutter of an eyelid. I gave him everything I knew, which was what I'd seen myself and what Waggish and the other detectives, Nappleby, Pason, Poireau, and Tourneur, had found out.

'Where is that paper now?' Beare asked when I had finished.

'I gave it to Waggish, like you said.'

'I want to see it. And I want to see the suspects. Please get them all here in an hour. Bring Miss Price here earlier. It is unlikely that she knows so little about her uncle as she claims.'

'The suspects?'

'Everyone who was there when the blackjack was stolen. Except Mr King: I take it that he has given all the information he had, and it would be tedious for him to watch another investigator's scratchwork.'

'You think the killer must be limited to that group?'

'No. The limitation is not absolute. Conceivably the person who took the weapon gave it to another person, and is lying about the theft not because he is guilty of murder, but from fear of the killer, or in hopes of blackmailing him.'

'If anyone but the murderer took it he's a sap not to say so. The murderer won't let him stay alive very much longer.'

Beare nodded. 'True. But then the suspects in this case do not appear to be distinguished by acumen. At any rate, while the limitation is not absolute it is the soundest working hypothesis. We cannot hold out for absolute truth; "he who would fix his condition upon incontestable reasons of preference must live and die inquiring and debating".'

I was on my way out, but I stopped. 'Confucius?'

Beare frowned.'Samuel Johnson.'

I brought Win along myself some time before the others were due. Beare was polite, explained that his failure to rise was not due to lack of courtesy, Then he got to work.

It turned out that of course she did know something about her uncle and his column, but none of it mattered. It was all old stuff, going back to the period before she'd left for France. She didn't know what he'd done in Paris, aside from breaking up her love life, and in London he'd been out most of the time while she moped around the hotel writing letters to Llewelyn.

I saw she was going to take a turn at the questions herself, but before she could the others began to arrive.

I got them seated somehow, borrowing chairs and squeezing myself on the end of Beare's berth.

It wasn't the group you'd have selected if you wanted a party, unless you hoped for another murder. Pictorially it had a wide range, from Win and Dolores Despana, neither of them open to any real criticism, to Homer T. Anderson at the other end of the spectrum, looking like something from a 3-D horror film. His face was cross and smug at the same time, if you can visualize that. Win was pale and jumpy. The Purser sat down near her and spent most of his time trying not to be too obvious about looking at her. The Doctor looked bored, and kept scribbling surreptitiously in a note-book. Mrs Chip-Ebberley had taken her usual precautions against being exposed to draughts, and she pulled her skirts in as if she didn't like her company; but, seeing she had Anderson on one side and Dolores, who'd accused her of murder, on the other, you couldn't really blame her for that. She brought out her knitting, but she didn't get any work done on it; whether it was because her hands were too shaky, I couldn't quite tell. The last to come in was the First Officer. He stared at Beare for a full thirty seconds, which was normal since it was their first meeting and Beare's four hundred pounds affected people that way. Then he realized he was being rude and got red under his tan. He looked away and gave me the paper, and I handed it to Beare.

Beare read it through twice. His face didn't change. After the second time through he folded it up and began his ques-tioning. He didn't mention the paper.

The most you could say for that session was that it killed a lot of time. Nobody contradicted anything he'd said before, and I couldn't see that anything new that came out was crucial. Nobody there had known anyone else on the ship before sailing. The only ones who had known Price before were Win, naturally, and Dolores whom he'd bought a drink or two. Even being on board the same ship, of course, didn't necessarily mean you'd had to meet him, and the fact was that of this group Beare and the First Officer had never exchanged a word with him; I had had just one short, but colourful exchange when he'd told me he was going to inter-view Beare and I'd told him the contrary, tersely; and the Doctor had spoken with him only a couple of times, when Price wanted medical attention. One time, he'd come by for a pill when he was sick, the Doctor explained –

Anderson made another of his unsolicited donations to the cause at that point. 'Yeah! And it wasn't just a medical visit, was it? It so happens I passed the door just then, and I heard him telling you off.' He turned to Beare. 'Price called him a no-good incompetent! I heard him.'

The Doctor drew himself up, and his face, which was definitely on the chubby side, looked more dignified than you'd have expected. 'He had very bad manners!' he exclaimed; his accent got so broad that he sounded like a Scotchman, which I gathered from the other Limeys was a sign of excitement in him.

'Manners!' Anderson was scornful.

Beare looked at him, his lips compressed, and refused to cross-examine the Doctor on the subject. I couldn't tell if it was because he disliked Anderson so much or because he really didn't take the Doctor seriously.

Mrs Chip-Ebberly, accused by Dolores of a mysterious connexion with Price, denied it cold. Any interest she had shown in him, she said, was due to his obvious involvement in a sinister matter which she could not discuss in public. There was no reason why he should have cut out her picture or followed her aboard. Beare couldn't break her down. Looking at her jaw, I decided no one could.

He didn't ask the Purser about his encounter with Price in the Lounge, and you could tell that Win was thankful for that.

There was only one question that took me by surprise: Beare asked Win, 'Did your uncle ever go to school in England?'

Her mouth fell open and she said: 'Why, no, he was never abroad before this trip. He went to school in Minnesota, the same as my father. It was the same school I went to myself when *I* was a kid, and I think it explains a lot in his personality; it was a *traumatic* experience for me – '

Beare cut off the reminiscences. 'Or in Canada?'

'No.'

After a while Beare sighed and looked at the torn page from Price's typewriter again. 'I should like you all to take part in a little exercise. Ernie! Will you please pass out pencils and paper?'

This took me completely by surprise, but I carried out the orders, dead-pan.

Beare said: 'Will you all be good enough to write the

following sentence at my dictation. "In the last election, the vote was 200 to 175 in favour of the Labour candidate." '

Right away there were some rumblings. Anderson sputtered: 'Crazy! What's the sense of all this?'

Mrs Chip-Ebberly looked past him as if the butler had made a mistake and shown the plumber into the drawing-room. 'Obviously', she said, 'It is a test of our handwriting. The purpose, I cannot fathom; but any innocent person will surely cooperate.'

I initialled their papers and passed them over to Beare. He looked through them briefly and stuck them inside his book. Then he started in on where the suspects had been last night at the time when we'd figured the paper must have been shoved under my cabin door. But when he was done I still didn't know who had done it.

Mrs Chip-Ebberly and Win had been in their cabins. Dolores Despana had been at the bar. A few minutes later it turned out that Anderson had been at the bar too, at the very same time. I gave Dolores an approving nod to show her I appreciated her taking my advice so soon, but she pretended not to notice.

The officers had been busy at work. By 'work' it appeared the Doctor meant writing his poem, not observing the Hippocratic oath; and to everyone's boredom Beare went off on a tangent with him, discussing rhyme schemes and metres and nodding sympathetically when the Doctor said he never read prose any longer lest it spoil his ear. I worked out a scheme for making Beare think the clue to the mystery was in that epic, so he'd have to read through all 57,000 lines, but I gave it up because he might have made me do the reading. Just as the Doctor was getting really worked up and offering to recite the Invocation and Canto One to our little gathering, a steward came to tell him he was needed in the sick-bay. He groaned and went out looking as if he would much rather stay and read to us.

Beare changed the subject again. I could tell he was just feeling around now. He turned to Win. 'Do you know what income your uncle received from his column?'

She shook her head.

I said, 'It seems he made more by what he *didn't* print than by what he did.' I don't usually butt in when Beare is at work, and this interruption was tactless since two and maybe more of the people in the room had been blackmailed by Price; but I hoped to get a rise out of Anderson. I didn't like the shape of his head.

But the one who reacted was Winifred. She cried out: 'You all think I'm awful for inheriting that kind of money. I know! I shouldn't take it! I won't take it! I'm not going to! It's *tainted!*' She looked at Mrs Chip-Ebberly, the only person in the room who looked as if she'd boggle over accepting coins with a few spots on them. Mrs Chip-Ebberly made motions indicating she thought the outburst was in bad taste; and watching Win in operation, I could see myself what Atlas Poireau had meant by calling her melodramatic. But then I saw the Purser watching her too, and from his expression you might have thought she was the heroine at the end of Act II, where she spurns the villain and his gold. I was interested, because any Purser who applauds that attitude towards money is miscast, and also, remembering how he'd flown out at Broderick Tourneur, I had a feeling something would go pop when Anderson, with a sneer at Win in her noble posture, threw another sneer in the direction of the Purser:

'You'll disappoint *some* people if you *don't* take it.'

Sure enough, the Purser jumped up ready to deliver a right to his jaw. I grabbed one arm and Mr Waggish got him by the other. His face was bright red, and he was breathing hard. Anderson was on his feet waving his arms about and gobbling: 'Look at him! He's a killer! He's the murderer!' With no particular logic to his timing, the Purser calmed down as quick as he'd got mad; and he only shrugged when Anderson refused to apologize. But while it lasted I'd never seen anyone look more as if he'd like to knock a head in.

That broke the party up. Nobody protested about going so soon. Following instructions from Beare, I kept Dolores back. She was all set to make a fuss about it, but then he showed her the paper. She was like a mother recovering her kidnapped child.

When he could pry her loose from it, Beare asked her if it was exactly the same as when she'd seen it in Price's type-writer. Had she read the other items through?

'*What* other items?' she asked. Then she got the point. She looked at the bottom half of the paper. First she said yes, it was the same, then she said no, she didn't think there had been quite so much written there. Then she said yes, and then no. . . . Then she got it into her head that if she said no, the whole works would be invalidated and her chance of getting the thing published would be lost, so she said positively, yes, it was exactly like that when she first saw it and she'd swear to that in any court.

Beare didn't say a word while she stood there making up her mind. At last, I took the paper from her gently but firmly, saying I'd take care of it, and propelled her through the door. I left the door open to clear the air and went back to Beare.

'Well,' I said enthusiastically, 'there are only two possibilities, yes or no. Either Price wrote that, or he didn't. Just go eeny, meeny, miny, mo – '

'Pfui. There was never any doubt that the bulk of the last paragraph is a forgery. The question was simply whether the forgery had taken place before Miss Despana entered Price's cabin.' He sighed again and looked around.

I knew it was beer he wanted, so I went into the bathroom for a glass. Then I heard him yell.

'Ernie!' His eyes were popping. He was pointing at the door. 'Someone reached in and took that scarf!'

The green box with all the Price exhibits was on the table just inside the door. I didn't stop to talk, but jumped to it, losing a little time because the way was jammed with extra chairs from our recent gathering. When I reached the door the thief was just in sight at the end of the passage, turning a corner. I tore after him, and would have caught up with him only one thing went wrong. I wasn't running on pavement, I was running on a deck that rocked up and down at a thirty-degree angle side-ways and a ten-degree angle back and forwards. I'd developed good enough sea legs to take that into account, even running; but I'd forgotten another factor. As I raced along something came up and caught my ankles. I crashed down, banged my forehead, and went out cold.

The next I knew, someone was screaming, 'Murder!' I managed to look up, and there were some dopey women. One of them said, 'Oh, he isn't dead, after all!' She sounded as if I had cheated them. I tried to make a suitable comment, but my head hurt. Then the Doctor was bending over me.

'That's a beautiful bruise,' he said.

I scrambled to my feet then, but my left ankle hurt like hell. The Doctor said to wait, but I preferred staggering to Beare's cabin to remaining on display in the operating theatre. I made it to his door, and fell into a chair.

Beare was on the edge of his bed, upright, clutching his safety-belt so he wouldn't fall off, and breathing hard. He did not say a word.

The Doctor had his bag with him. He put a plaster on my head, and felt my ankle. 'Just a strain,' he said. 'You'd better not use it for a day or so. . . . You know it's *dangerous* to run on board ship, Mr Woodbin.' He sounded reproachful.

'I was chasing a thief. You got there pretty quick.'

'I was just around the corner in the crew's quarters, with my patients.'

'It's funny you didn't see the guy I was chasing. He was headed that way.'

He shook his head. 'I did hear someone running by, but it was two or three minutes before I came out into the passageway and saw you lying on deck.'

Beare said, fuming: 'What the devil happened?'

The Doctor said, 'Mr Woodbin isn't used to ships. He forgot to pick up his feet when he came to a bulkhead, so he tripped and fell on his face.'

Beare frowned at me. 'You were not struck down?'

'No.' I was curt. 'I don't think so. It was one of those bulkheads that stick up a few inches. I forgot that a race on shipboard would be a steeplechase.'

I was still furious with myself, but Beare was sympathetic; it was proof for him of the danger of stirring from a berth. The Doctor said he was sorry too, as if he meant it, and he went out promising Beare to ask the First Officer to stop by at his earliest convenience.

Beare asked. 'Could you see who it was?'

I shook my head carefully on account of the throbbing. 'He was short, he wore a light jacket. It could have been a steward – or someone in a steward's coat. He headed towards the door to the crew's quarters, as if he knew where he was going. And *he* didn't forget to pick up his feet. He capered like a goddam mountain goat.'

The First Officer let out a whistle when he saw my head. He said he was sorry; but I got the impression it wasn't only personal sympathy – rather, a feeling also that I'd let him down. He told Beare he was trying to check on the crew now. He looked at Beare uncertainly.

Beare said: 'We had better discuss this preposterous fraud.' He tapped the gossip-sheet from Price's machine.

The First Officer was startled. 'Fraud? What do you mean, Mr Beare?'

Beare waggled a finger. 'You recognized it yourself, sir. Subconsciously, at any rate. When Mr Woodbin showed you the paper you said it was "daft".'

'Aye.' Mr Waggish nodded emphatically.

Beare inclined his head. 'The first two paragraphs I take to be genuine. Mr Price typed them. The last one is, on the whole, sheer flummery; the latter part of it was typed by someone other than Mr Price – presumably after his death. Presumably too, the second typist was the intruder who tore the paper from the machine. As to the contents of the paragraphs, it is pure gibberish and an attempt to confuse.'

'Then it's of no use to us?'

'On the contrary. It may help us to limit the number of suspects. On the basis of this forgery, I am inclined to eliminate Miss Despana, Miss Price, and Mr Anderson.'

I had figured this out by now, but I didn't wonder that The First Officer didn't get it. He stared at Beare and asked, 'How?'

'The style', Beare told us, 'is a tolerable imitation of Price's even as it disintegrates into nonsense. That suggests an American as forger. But observe this word.' He pointed: ' "Colour." That is the British spelling. When I dictated, just now, the analogous words "labour" and "favour", the Britishers in the group spelled them, as one would expect, "o-u-r"; the Americans "o-r". And, more conclusive to my mind, the word "whilst" is used where an American would, without exception, say "while".'

'Oh, I see – Good heavens!' The First Officer looked respectful, and I was glad that Beare at least had come up to expectations. 'I never would have known that.'

'No. Precisely. An Englishman would not notice. An American would.'

'Then it must be one of the Britishers who wrote the forgery!'

'Not "must", sir. It may be an American subtle enough to have adopted British usage in hopes of bamboozling us. Theoretically, that is possible.' Beare sighed. 'But in actual fact, which of them could have done so? Anderson, a Caliban who has been given electric buttons to push? Miss Price, an immature schoolgirl? Miss Despana, a – '

'Siren?' I suggested.

'No.'

'Houri?'

'A barbarian. No. Or at least . . . Confound it!' Beare was peevish. 'The obvious inference is that one of *you* gentlemen, Mr Waggish, or Mrs Chip-Ebberly, is responsible for this mess.'

'That helps a lot,' I said brightly.

'But I resent the obvious.' Beare scowled. 'I want to think.'

He sat up against his pillows, eyes closed, and he began to suck his lips in and then pop them out again. I felt myself get tense. I'd explained to the First Officer how I always looked forward to this stage in an investigation. When Beare did that with his mouth it meant he was beginning to let his mind work. It meant he might come up with an answer. Mr Waggish looked puzzled as minutes passed, and then, looking at me, he remembered. His face brightened, and he looked at Beare as if he hoped for an answer this time. We both sat there watching.

Finally Beare let out a good loud pop. He opened his eyes.

'Ernie,' he said. 'Please ring for the steward. I want some beer.'

CHAPTER 9

MISS FAN SLIVER

'This is a fine, pleasant sight. It makes the ship seem quite homelike.' The First Officer smiled down at Miss Fan Sliver as she sat quietly, knitting, in a straight-backed chair in the Lounge. It was a short time before Mr Trajan Beare's conference.

Miss Sliver beamed at him. 'How kind of you to say so!'

He inspected the soft, fuzzy white strip which hung from her needles. 'A – a sweater, is it, ma'am?' he asked.

'An infant's vest.' Miss Sliver explained that a niece had just had quadruplets, and that she hoped to have a set of warm garments for each baby by the time she returned to England. 'I shall be kept busy, but I should really not have felt justified in a holiday trip, were it not that this sort of work can be carried on whilst one travels.'

Mr Waggish laughed. 'Sailors have been known to knit too, Miss Sliver, but it's entirely out of *my* line. I never thought that I should have the job of investigating a woollen muffler!'

'A muffler?' Miss Sliver looked up with an air of expectant interest.

Mr Waggish surveyed her as she sat there. No one could have seemed more prim and dull. Her mousy hair was unruffled by sea-breezes. In fact, Miss Sliver had scarcely ventured on deck – 'so damp, and so draughty', she had explained to Mrs Chip-Ebberly, '*aside* from the risk of slipping and falling overboard!' Her pince-nez was attached to her dress by a thick black ribbon; she wore woollen stockings and buttoned boots. All in all, she was the incarnation of a retired governess. She reminded Mr Waggish of a dear old

114

aunt of his in Bath. He said apologetically, 'But it's not a very nice subject to discuss in front of a lady.'

Miss Sliver permitted herself a faint smile. 'My profession has brought me into contact with many instances of unpleasantness and, I regret to say, of violence.'

'That's true.' Mr Waggish was abashed. 'I knew you were a detective, of course, Miss Sliver, but it's hard to remember. That is, you – I mean to say-' He broke off, a little red in the face.

Miss Sliver said kindly, 'The muffler you allude to is, I dare say, the one found near Mr Price's body? A dreadful affair.'

'Aye, that's the one. A red and yellow scarf. It was on deck, you see, under the body, along with a pipe. The pipe seems to have been taken from the store; anyone could have taken it. But we cannot trace that muffler. I wish you'd look at it, Miss Sliver! Maybe, *you* could tell us something about it.'

Miss Sliver smiled. 'I have seen it; on the morning of the discovery. I recall it well. But beyond the obvious facts that it is of Midlands yarn – number 6 or 7, I should say – and of pre-war quality, I fear I can be of little assistance to you.'

Mr Waggish said: 'There is no shop label, so we couldn't trace it in that way, even if we were ashore. I suppose it was torn off.'

Miss Sliver coughed. 'My dear Mr Waggish! The scarf is obviously of *home* manufacture.'

'Ah? You are sure of that?'

'It is quite beyond doubt. In any case – '

A steward interrupted with a low-voiced message for the First Officer. He turned to Miss Sliver to excuse himself.

Miss Sliver smiled. 'Pray do not let me detain you.'

As he left, she shivered a little, and realized that this section of the Lounge was now exposed to draught; some porthole had been opened. . . . Really *most* reckless. She rose, holding her knitting and her flowered knitting bag carefully in one hand and keeping the other free to grip tables and chairs should the rolling of the *Florabunda* increase.

Crossing the Lounge, Miss Sliver paused more than once to nod to friends. In these few days at sea she had made several most interesting acquaintances. In that respect the trip had proved even more broadening, more stimulating, more rewarding than she had hoped. There was Professor Cheetah with his tales – 'instructive, yet so entertaining' – of excavations in Syria. There were the Thistlethwaites, who had turned out to be friends of very old and dear friends of Miss Sliver's in Dorset. 'Such a small world, is it not?' There was Mr Ernie Woodbin, with his fund of information about orchids and his interesting American idiom.

The only drawback, in fact, to the voyage was the distressing series of incidents arising first from Paul Price's reprehensible life, and then from his death. As hours went by and the criminal remained at large, tension mounted. It was not pleasant to think that one of the persons about one might be guilty of so shocking a crime.

Miss Sliver nodded kindly to a young steward who was slipping unobtrusively past. 'A chilly afternoon, is it not?'

He gulped. 'Yes, miss,' he said.

Miss Sliver sighed as he vanished. Such a pleasant lad! A mere boy – surely no more than sixteen. She had chatted with him on the first evening out, drawing him out in her inimitable way. It was his first trip, and he was filled with excitement! But now he, like the passengers, was affected by the knowledge that a murderer was at large. He was pale and nervous and had lost his high spirits.

No one, indeed, was quite at ease. The community of passengers resembled a village, Miss Sliver thought. There was the same limited range of interests, the same tendency to accept the easy and popular attitude towards any given event; above all, the same insatiable curiosity and love of gossip. She found a specimen of this gossip as she passed a group of middle-aged women playing bridge near the fireplace. She caught the words 'shocking' and 'unfair', and then: ' . . . they say they have all the evidence against her that is needed, but because she's *who she is* they won't arrest her!'

Miss Sliver frowned. The story of the boat-drill, and of Miss Dolores Despana's charges against the Hon. Mrs Chip-Ebberley, had spread rapidly. People who had courted Mrs Chip-Ebberley from snobbish motives now shunned her and whispered behind her back. She was not a woman to whom Miss Sliver was attracted: she was large, rigid, and overbearing in person, and narrow, rigid, and overbearing in opinion. But Miss Sliver was eminently just and temperate.

Her sense of fairness was offended by the readiness of the passengers at large to give credence to a quite unprovable accusation – particularly as the ladies, at least, were illogical enough to shun Miss Despana herself, and Miss Price, as well!

With a pleasant nod, Miss Sliver took a seat near Mrs Chip-Ebberly. She wondered a little at her choosing to place herself in so public a room; but *courage*, she reminded herself, must be esteemed! Mrs Chip-Ebberly was clearly not at ease. Her eyes darted about the Lounge, and though her knitting-bag, flowered like Miss Sliver's, lay on a table beside her, and a large ball of light-grey wool and needles with an inch of light-grey ribbing in her lap, she scarcely pretended to knit. For long periods her hands remained quite still.

Miss Sliver came to the end of her ball of white wool. She extracted a new skein from her knitting-bag.

Winifred Price came near. She was with the Purser. She looked about rather defiantly at the other passengers, who broke off their talk at her approach; but she looked like a fluffy kitten who is lost and unhappy. Miss Sliver was fond of young girls. She greeted this one kindly, and the dark eyes responded gratefully. Winifred asked:

'May I help you wind that yarn, Miss Sliver?'

Miss Sliver was pleased to note that, in spite of the emotional ordeal she was undergoing, the young American was well-mannered. She smiled with peculiar graciousness. 'How very kind of you to offer! If you would really not mind holding the skein, it would be most helpful!'

Winifred Price took a seat opposite her, and held up her hands for the skein. Turning to Mrs Chip-Ebberly, she said politely, but in evident nervousness of the older lady: 'The Purser has been telling me some stories about his work – the things he has to do!'

'Well, its worse since the war,' said the Purser. He was evidently continuing their previous conversation.

Winifred Price said: 'It must be *terribly* hard to travel on only fifty pounds! It's a wonder that the British are able to travel at all!'

Mrs Chip-Ebberly sniffed. 'Hard! It is intolerable, Miss Price. One had never expected that one would be required to travel on an allowance, as if one were a child!' She looked to Miss Sliver for agreement.

Miss Sliver coughed. She said mildly: 'Doubtless the currency restrictions do cause great awkwardness and even, I fear, hardship in individual cases.'

The Purser's lips twitched. He said. 'You'd be suprised, Miss Sliver, how easily some people get over that awkwardness. There are plenty of clever dodges – too clever by half. If they don't actually smuggle sterling out, they take out valuables.'

'How romantic *smuggling* sounds!' exclaimed Winifred Price.'Like pirates and highwaymen, and outlaws!'

Miss Sliver coughed again. There was a hint of reproof in her voice as she observed: 'My dear Miss Price! We must not let the superficial colourfulness of such activities blind us to the gravely mistaken ingenuity which makes them possible. To smuggle is, after all, to commit a felony.'

The tone was that in which, in the schoolroom, she had corrected many an errant boy or girl.

Winifred Price blushed. 'Oh, I know, it's anti-social,' she said, 'And I'm honestly not criminally inclined, Miss Sliver. I accounted for every franc I spent, on that Customs form we had to fill out; and *still* I'm nervous about going through Customs!'

The Purser said, 'They're only interested in professional crooks, you know. Dope, diamonds, and liquor – and they're usually tipped off in advance whom to look for. They've a good eye for such things. If you've a secret stock of cocaine, Miss Winifred, you had better make a clean breast of it before we dock. Just come to my office and confess!'

Winifred Price laughed. She looked more alive, more the way a girl of her age should look, than she had before. Miss Sliver gazed at her benignly. A charming girl. And the Purser, so very handsome and . . . Miss Sliver sighed. She hoped, with a faint twinge of anxiety, that neither young person had allowed *proximity*, and the *peculiar* circumstances of the voyage, to lead him or her to mistake a natural friendship for something more!

Mrs Chip-Ebberly was speaking. She said portentously: 'I do not consider crime a jesting matter. Let us change the subject. I – '

118

'*What's that?*' Winifred Price asked sharply, starting nervously and pointing to the table. Her interruption, and her manner, showed Miss Sliver that her gaiety was only momentary. Underneath lay deep uneasiness, even fear.

She was pointing at an object which a sudden motion of the ship had dislodged from behind Mrs. Chip-Ebberly's knitting-bag. It was a gleaming cigarette-case.

'What a beauty!' the Purser exclaimed.

Mrs Chip-Ebberly picked it up and looked at it suspiciously. 'It is a very *expensive* case,' she said. 'Someone was exceedingly careless to leave it lying about. Such cases should not be left lying about. They are positive inducements to crime!'

The Purser said cheerfully: 'You're absolutely right, Mrs Chip-Ebberly. If people would only deposit their valuables with me, we'd be spared a lot of trouble. I wonder who left this loose. They'll be running to me in the morning to say it's stolen.'

Miss Sliver coughed. 'I believe the case belongs to Miss Despana. I have observed her using one very like it. And she sat here earlier today.'

Mrs Chip-Ebberly put the case down as if it had burned her fingers. The air was instantly thick with her dislike.

Winfred Price said quickly: 'Miss Despana? Why, she's coming over here now! She must be looking for it.'

The Purser forgot himself to the point of letting out a very low, foreboding whistle. He looked enormously uncomfortable as Miss Sliver and Mrs Chip-Ebberly looked up at him in deprecation.

Dolores Despana asked: 'Did anyone see a cigarette-case here?' She saw Mrs Chip-Ebberly, and gave a start. An odd expression crossed her face as their eyes met. She seemed unable to tear her eyes away: it was as if she were a gorgeous varicoloured bird, hypnotized by some drabber but more powerful foe.

Miss Sliver watched the encounter gravely, without a pause in the rhythmical clicking of her needles. She said, with her usual ready tact: 'A beautiful cigarette-case. Most exquisite workmanship! We have just been admiring it. It is of French manufacture, Miss Despana?'

Dolores Despana finally freed her gaze from Mrs Chip-

Ebberly. Picking up her case, she said indifferently: 'I don't know. A gentleman friend of mine in New York gave it to me; it's solid gold.'

The Purser said genially: 'It's much too fine to leave about like that, Miss Despana. Not safe.'

'*Safe!*' Dorores Despana repeated indignantly. She had, Miss Sliver noted with regret, no desire to preserve a decent semblance of ordinary social intercourse. 'Nothing's safe on this ship. Not even your *life*.' She looked significantly at Mrs Chip-Ebberly, this time without losing her courage, and after a moment added in a trembling, loudish voice: 'If those detectives were any good they'd have the killer under lock and key by now. If you ask me, they're just so many phonies.'

Winifred Price's eyes sparkled with anger. She said, 'Don't you know Miss Sliver is a detective herself?'

Miss Despana stared at Miss Sliver. 'You?' she asked. 'You're a detective? Somebody said you were, but I thought they were pulling my leg.' Her round blue eyes took in the hair-net, the fringe, the dowdy dress and woollen stockings. She added, 'I thought you must be a schoolteacher.'

Miss Sliver said quietly: 'For many years I was engaged in the scholastic profession. But I am now a private investigator.'

'Well, what do you know!' Miss Despana observed faintly; she already seemed to have lost interest in the subject. Her eyes wandered across the room. Glimpsing the unattractive form of Mr Homer T. Anderson, she brightened. She nodded casually to Miss Sliver and directed a defiant stare at Mrs Chip-Ebberly. Then she walked away very gracefully. A moment later the Purser excused himself.

Mrs Chip-Ebberly had been sitting stiffly upright in an attitude of almost inhuman rigour. Now she relaxed. The ball of grey wool slid from her lap to the deck, and rolled away. Winifred Price slipped a hand free of the white skein she was holding for Miss Sliver, and reached for the ball; but, stooping from her chair, Mrs Chip-Ebberly almost snatched it from the girl's fingers. She cried in a sharp voice: 'Pray don't trouble!'

Winifred looked both startled and disconcerted. She gasped a little.

Mrs Chip-Ebberly bit her lip, evidently recognizing that she had been discourteous. 'Thank you very much,' she said. 'I did not want you to lose your skein, and have to disentangle it. I – I fear my nerves are not what they should be.'

Miss Sliver said brightly: 'I have been admiring your wool, Mrs Chip-Ebberly. Such an interesting shade. So soft, so tasteful. It is to be a scarf?'

'Yes.' Mrs Chip-Ebberly thrust the ball and the long needles, with their edging of grey, into her flowered bag. 'I have letters to write,' she said, rising. Her eyes turned in the direction which Miss Despana had taken, and she said: 'Should anything happen to me, it is well that there should be a *record!* There is, after all, more than my own fate at stake! Pray forgive me if I leave you.'

Winifred Price watched her go. She said suddenly: 'I hate this trip!' Her eyes filled with tears.

Miss Sliver coughed. 'You have had a most unfortunate experience, my dear Miss Price.'

'The whole atmosphere is ghastly. We all suspect each other. Do you think Mrs Chip-Ebberly tried to kill Dolores, Miss Sliver?'

'I think that Miss Despana genuinely believes that she did.'

'But do *you* think so?'

Miss Sliver said gravely: 'I do not know. It would be easy, if one were frightened, and with the motion of the ship, and the steepness of the ladder, to imagine that one had been pushed from behind . . . If Mrs Chip-Ebberly did do it, it was an exceedingly *rash* act, as well as a wicked one!'

Winifred Price wrinkled her nose thoughtfully. 'Well, I can't make up my own mind about it. If she did push her, then I suppose she's the murderer, too. And she is so very *respectable* that you can't help suspecting her. She is obviously dangerously repressed! Inhibited!'

Miss Sliver put down her knitting, shocked. She gazed at Winifred Price. 'My dear child!'

Winifred Price said hastily: 'Well, she's so – aristocratic. Some people seem to think she's above suspicion just because she has a title. Of course, I know that isn't what *you* mean – '

Miss Sliver's cough rebuked her again. 'Most decidedly not! As Lord Tennyson so admirably put it:

'Howe'er it be, it seems to me,
'Tis only noble to be good.

121

Kind hearts are more than coronets,
        And simple faith than Norman blood.'

Miss Price listened, Miss Sliver observed regretfully, with a
polite but rather blank expression. When Miss Sliver had
concluded, she said:

'Anyway, I'd rather believe *Dolores* is guilty. Mrs Chip-
Ebberly seems just as suspicious of her as she is of Mrs Chip-
Ebberly! She might have done it with Mr Anderson as an
accessory, or the other way around; they're as thick as thieves
just now. Of course, she's on the make.'

Miss Sliver said quietly: 'We ought not to think ill if we
can help it.'

'I know,' Winifred dropped her hands as Miss Sliver wound
the last of the white yarn neatly about her ball. 'I expect
really I'm just catty about her because of submerged sexual
jealousy, she's so pretty!' As Miss Sliver frowned in distress,
she continued hurriedly: 'You're probably right, Miss Sliver.
She probably is only interested in Mr Anderson because she
hopes he will be an angel.'

Miss Sliver's charitable proclivities had not carried her so
far that she could envisage this possibility. She cried in mild
bewilderment: 'An angel? Really, my dear Miss Price, I hardly
dare hope – '

Winifred Price gurgled with laughter. Then she said quite
nicely: 'I beg your pardon, Miss Sliver. I *am* sorry. But that's
American slang; it simply means that she wants him to finance
a show for her.' Her face sobered, and she said, 'If my uncle
was – was murdered for money, that might have something
to do with it.' She looked at Miss Sliver questioningly, in
helpless awareness of her own confusion.

Miss Sliver said quietly: 'I think financial issues do, indeed,
play a part in this case. But not, perhaps, in quite the way
you mean!'

Miss Sliver was a little late at the next meal. Slipping into
her seat, she apologized to her table-companions.

'Pray forgive me – '

She was cut off by a babel of voices.

'Have you heard the latest, Miss Sliver? Mr Woodbin has
been assaulted!'

122

'He was struck down whilst pursuing the killer!'

'They say he is at death's door!'

Miss Sliver saw that the place next hers, Mr Woodbin's, was empty. The young steward passed it now, and gave her the menu with trembling hands.

'Thick soup, please.' Miss Sliver looked quietly about at the excited faces.

Mrs Thistlethwaite declared: 'If this goes on, we won't dare leave our cabins! It is certainly a maniac.'

Mr Thistlethwaite nodded, and said with great authoritativeness: 'If Mr Woodbin should die of his injuries, it will be *murder!*'

There was a choking sound behind Miss Sliver. A small flood of thick brownish soup spilled from the plate the steward was handing her, and trickled over the white tablecloth.

'Sorry, miss!' he gasped. He patted his napkin over the spot, greatly agitated, and withdrew. When he came back with a fresh white square of linen, Miss Sliver watched his fumbling hands cover the stained place and rearrange the cutlery. She said:

'The report has been much exaggerated. I have just seen the Doctor – that is why I am late. Mr Woodbin tripped on a bulkhead, and fell. He has strained his ankle. It is unfortunate, of course, and, I fear, very painful. He must exercise great caution. But it is, I am happy to say, decidedly not fatal.'

As a chorus of cries and questions arose, she added gravely: 'I think one must beware of fostering the spread of rumours. So easy to lead to exaggeration! This soup is really excellent, is it not?'

The meal continued on a more cheerful level. Miss Sliver rose from table conversing of the film which was to be shown that evening. At the door she stopped, and exclaimed: 'I have left my handkerchief behind! Dear me!' Excusing herself, she crossed the dining-saloon to her table. The steward was piling saucers on his tray. He turned a round, startled face to her and stammered:

'Can I help you, miss?'

Miss Sliver retrieved the handkerchief which she had had the forethought to leave on her chair. She looked at him soberly and said: 'I thought that *I* could perhaps be of assistance to *you!*'

He stammered: 'I – I don't know what you mean, miss, I – '

Miss Sliver said, 'If you have done nothing wrong, you know, there is nothing to be afraid of.'

She continued to gaze at him expectantly. She smiled. It was the smile with which she had been wont, in the schoolroom, to encourage the shy and the timid. This boy was not proof against it.

'Oh, miss,' he said in a whisper. 'I don't know what to do, and that's the truth.'

'You had better tell me about it. Can you come to my stateroom after you have finished your work?'

'It's against the rules, miss.'

Miss Sliver said: 'I will take the responsibility with your superiors. I think that on this occasion we have the right to waive minor regulations. Perhaps, indeed, it is our *duty* to do so!'

The young steward sat gingerly on the edge of a chair in Miss Sliver's cabin. She looked at him kindly over her knitting. 'Well, Bert – You did say your name is Bert Higgs, did you not?'

'Yes, Please, miss, is it true that Mr Woodbin is not hurt bad?' He looked at her with intense anxiety.

'Quite true.'

He gave a sigh of relief.

'It was you whom Mr Woodbin was chasing when he fell, was it not?' She looked at him invitingly.

'How did you know?' he gasped.

Miss Sliver coughed. 'It is evident that your concern for Mr Woodbin's health goes beyond the ordinary. Indeed, you have appeared worried and unhappy ever since the murder was discovered.'

Bert Higgs's eyes grew bigger. He said imploringly: 'I didn't do the murder, miss! I didn't do him in! I never spoke to the gent.'

Miss Sliver folded her hands in her lap. She said: 'Suppose you tell me all about it.'

Bert Higgs gazed at her there with her knitting, with her

knick-knacks and photographs about her. He was suddenly reminded of his Sunday-school teacher back in Liverpool. The words came out in a rush: 'Well, miss, it all began with that muffler. It's mine, that muffler is!' He looked at her expecting signs of astonishment, but Miss Sliver merely continued to gaze at him with benignant inquiry. 'I left it somewhere, miss. It dropped in a passageway, most like. And I didn't ever see it again till — Well, I heard it was found on deck with the dead body, and they began asking questions, and though I knew it must be my muffler I was afraid to say so.'

'You were very wrong not to report ownership at once. The needless questioning has delayed the inquiry, and may have caused sad confusion.'

Bert Higgs gulped. 'Yes, miss.'

'When did you realize that it was missing?'

'The day before the gent was killed, miss. But I might have lost it earlier. I can't rightwise remember.'

'And you cannot remember where you left it?'

'No, miss, unless I dropped it in a passage as I said, where anyone could have picked it up.'

'And you tried to recover it today. Why did you do that, Bert?'

'I thought I could get it back and throw it overboard; and then Mr Woodbin saw me and ran after me. . . . I never meant him to get hurt!'

For a moment Miss Sliver said nothing. Then she asked: 'Why were you so afraid?'

'It's *my muffler*, miss!'

'But you could not suppose that *that* would be enough to make the authorities suspect you of murder. You have not told me quite everything, have you?'

The rest came forth quickly. Bert Higgs looked at her as if she were a sorceress. He said, with anxious eyes: 'No, miss. The fact is, I never spoke to Mr Price, but I once heard him talking, see? It was at night, and I was — I was on the boat-deck.' He gulped again and raised his eyes to her in despair. 'I'm not allowed to be there, see? But I — I wanted to see the ship, like, so I crept up there when it was dark, and there was that Mr Price, what was killed, talking to a lady near a lifeboat!'

'What lady?'

'I don't know who she was, miss. I didn't see them. He said: "You act mighty fine, but I know about that ice." She says. "Ice?" all puzzled like, and he says, "Yeah, ice!" like that. "*Yeah, ice!*" '

Bert Higgs quoted these words with a sort of leer, speaking through the side of his mouth. His mimicry confirmed a notion which had been vaguely forming itself in Miss Sliver's mind. She said: 'So you feared that your knowledge of a secret conversation of Mr Price's would bring you under suspicion?'

'That's it, miss! I know too much! I was scared of the coppers. The *dicks!*'

'I see. You go to the cinema often when you are at home, Bert, I dare say? Is that how you knew that the "dicks" would assume that you were guiltily involved?'

'Yes, miss, the flicks, that's right, but it's they thrillers, too.'

'Ah, you read detective stories? In the ship's library?'

'Yes, miss, and Westerns! There's a big chest of them, miss; they come down from the bridge for us.'

Miss Sliver sighed. She said: 'I think you will find that the gentlemen in charge of this investigation are not like the "dicks" you are afraid of. I shall have to inform them of this, of course, but I shall explain, too, why you have acted as you did.'

Miss Sliver knitted thoughtfully for some moments after Bert Higgs had left. Then, with an air of decision, she rang for the stewardess and sent a message to the First Officer, asking if she might see him as soon as convenient.

She knocked at the door of the next cabin. Mrs Chip-Ebberly received her with evident surprise, and asked her to be seated.

'Has something new happened?' she demanded. 'Has there been another attack?'

'None, I am happy to say. There has, however, been a development in the progress of the inquiry.'

Mrs Chip-Ebberly said vigorously: 'Good! Excellent! I trust they will apprehend the criminal at once! This suspense is more than vexatious, and a delay in landing would be intolerable.'

Miss Sliver said quietly: 'It has been discovered that Mr Price had learned that a certain passenger was removing diamonds illegally from the United Kingdom, in order to convert them into dollars. He informed this passenger of his knowledge. His purpose, presumably, was blackmail.'

Mrs Chip-Ebberly sat like a statue. Her eyes were glued to Miss Sliver's.

Miss Sliver added: 'His threats to expose his victim provided a motive for murder.'

Mrs Chip-Ebberly's face broke. She cried: 'Murder? No! Certainly not!'

Miss Sliver regarded her levelly. There was no word spoken for a long moment. Then she said: 'It is unlikely that the smuggling scheme would have succeeded, in any case. The method is extremely amateurish.' Her eyes dropped to Mrs Chip-Ebberly's knitting-bag. 'One likes to think that it was a misguided impulse, under financial strain, and that the malefactor would have repented before the time came for the consummation of the plan. The authorities might, if it were freely admitted before reaching port, be lenient.'

Miss Sliver rose and went to the door. 'Good night, Mrs Chip-Ebberly,' she said.

Mr Waggish jumped up and handed Miss Sliver to a chair. 'This is a pleasure and an honour, ma'am. Does this visit mean that you have trapped the killer?'

Miss Sliver's faint shade of coolness reproved this frivolity. 'As I said earlier, I do not wish to engage in the investigation. It would be presumptuous and, I am sure, unnecessary. But one or two facts have come to my attention, and it is my duty to lay them before you.'

Mr Waggish looked at her quizzically. 'I'm all ears, Miss Sliver.'

'Mr Price had discovered that one of the passengers was smuggling diamonds into the United States, with the intention of establishing an illegal stock of dollars there.'

The smile left Mr Waggish's face. He bent forward alertly. 'Smuggling!' he repeated. '*Who?*'

Miss Sliver coughed. 'Mrs Chip-Ebberly'

He sat back, incredulous. 'Mrs Chip-Ebberly? Are you sure?'

'I fear it is all too certain. On the first night out, I observed that Mr Price was unduly interested in her. He spied on her in her cabin. We know from Miss Price that he sailed on this ship because Mrs Chip-Ebberly was to be aboard. Tonight, I learned that he was overheard threatening to expose a "lady". You will recall Mr Anderson's telling Mr Jerry Pason that Mr Price had said it would be a profitable trip, with the cryptic addition that he "hated the water except for the ice". "Ice" is, of course, an American colloquialism for *diamonds*. It is the sort of language, and the sort of witticism, in which Mr Price indulged. How he discovered Mrs Chip-Ebberly's plan in the first place, I do not know; but he had agents here and there, and since the plan could not have been worked out without the consent of some members of her family at least, several persons must have known of it, and the chances of leakage have been considerable. Mr Price apparently knew the people involved only by name: I expect that the picture he clipped from the *Tatler* was for purposes of identification. Mrs Chip-Ebberly's hostility to the detectives, and some aspects of her rather odd behaviour in general, can be explained, I think, on the grounds of her guilty conscience.'

'I can still hardly believe it,' Mr Waggish said feebly. 'She is – Has she admitted it?'

'Not explicitly.'

There was a *rat-tat-tat* at the door. Without waiting for a summons the Purser entered. His boyish face was quite pink with excitement. 'Oh, here you are!' he cried to the First Officer.'You'll never guess what's happened!'

Seeing Miss Sliver, he broke off; but Mr Waggish motioned him to continue. 'Well – Mrs Chip-Ebberly just came to see me. She told me that, as the result of a conversation we'd had earlier, she wished to deposit something in my safe, to be held for her return trip to England!'

The Purser brought his hand dramatically from his pocket. There was a flash of light. Mr Waggish gave a low whistle. Miss Sliver sighed a little.

The Purser went on ironically: 'She told me she had "forgotten" that she had this with her, till she came across it in her valise. If you can imagine "forgetting" a necklace worth thousands of pounds!'

Mr Waggish looked at Miss Sliver with profound respect. He asked: 'How did you guess it?'

Miss Sliver coughed. 'It was not precisely "guessing", Mr Waggish. I have already mentioned some of my reasons. I observed that, though Mrs Chip-Ebberly carried knitting about constantly, she actually accomplished very little. That might have meant nothing, to be sure. But today she was inordinately anxious to prevent Miss Price from handling her ball of wool when it fell from her lap; and she betrayed great constraint when the talk turned on smuggling – whilst you were there, Purser. Knowing of the family jewels, I guessed she might be concealing something in her ball in an attempt to evade the currency restrictions. Her plan was, of course, a sadly *crude* and *unprofessional* one. It is hard to fancy how she expected to deceive the Customs officials?'

Mr Waggish agreed. 'That's it! She is not an – an *actress*, is she? I cannot see her as a murderer.'

Miss Sliver said in her equable way: 'I do not say that she is one. I simply do not know.'

'*Who* overheard the conversation with Price, by the way?'

'It was a young steward, Bert Higgs.'

The Purser cried: 'What? And he didn't tell us before?'

Mr Waggish looked at Miss Sliver with an odd combination of affection, amusement, and awe. He said: 'I think Miss Sliver has something up her sleeve.'

Miss Sliver said: 'My dear Mr Waggish!'

Mr Waggish apologized for the flippancy.

Miss Sliver resumed: 'Bert Higgs is the owner of the red and yellow muffler.'

The two officers gasped.

'But you don't – Do you mean the lad is the killer?' Mr Waggish asked.

'I am quite certain that he is not. His scarf was stolen.'

The Purser said: 'But why would anyone want to steal someone else's scarf and leave it at the scene of a crime? The kid must have *some* connexion with the murder!'

Miss Sliver said quietly: 'A more important question is, why any muffler at *all* was left there, the murderer's or another's.'

'If he's innocent, why the deuce didn't he come and tell us?' the Purser insisted.

Miss Sliver said earnestly: 'Because he is very young, and his head is stuffed with detective novels. The result is that he has a most unfortunate conception of murder investigations!'

The First Officer said in some embarrassment, 'Why, but I read thrillers myself.' He looked at Miss Sliver like one of her pupils caught in a misdeed.

Miss Sliver coughed. 'But you read them, I trust, in a different spirit, my dear Mr Waggish!' She looked at the officers gravely. 'Believe me, I cannot think that this boy is guilty, and I trust that the investigation will not be deflected from its true course on his account. If it is, it will happen that, as Lord Tennyson prophesied of another Quest:

> 'This chance of noble deeds will come and go
> Unchallenged, while ye follow wandering fires,
> Lost in the quagmire!'

Mr Waggish looked at her with reverence. 'I think it's remarkable, Miss Sliver, the way you've detected. To think of you just sitting so quietly, knitting away and uncovering a smuggling plot, and finding the owner of that muffler – who is in *our* department, too, so to speak, being in the crew – knitting away whilst villains are foiled. Knitting like those ladies in the stories – '

The Purser offered, nodding: 'Like that Madame Defarge, or whatever, do you mean, in the Dickens book, who sat at the foot of the guillotine and knitted a stitch for every head that fell?'

Miss Sliver's hands fell to her lap. She coughed in unmistakable reproof. She exclaimed with mild severity: 'My dear Purser! Surely not, I trust, quite like *that!*'

Mr Waggish looked at the Purser in disgust. He explained, 'I meant the *Fates*, knitting away and settling what will happen to chaps on earth.'

Miss Sliver said in kindly correction: 'My dear Mr Waggish! It was, I believe, *spinning* rather than *knitting* which was attributed to the Fates! And, in any case, I have settled nothing. Indeed, as I see it, the mystery is nearly as puzzling as it was three days ago!'

CHAPTER 10

SPIKE BLUDGEON

(*From his memoirs*)

The fog was like sweat, grey and damp and beady, and the ocean was like the grey cold gravy you get in Bowery hash-houses. Looking in from the deck, the lights in the Lounge were warm and pretty, like twinkly bulbs on a Christmas tree, till you thought about the ship and you saw what it really was, a rotton tub with a cargo of dirt. Human dirt. A floating sewer. The *Florabunda*. A place where murder had been done.

And I was the guy who must catch the killer.

The case wouldn't have dragged on this long, only I'd been out of commission for the last few days, since the night before the murder was discovered. I'd been hit by a pain that jabbed my body through and through till I ached in every bone and every muscle, a pain that churned my guts and made me want to die. . . . The ship's Doctor said it was seasickness, and at the time I took his word for it. Later, looking back over events, I questioned that diagnosis and with good reason.

Anyway, now I was on my feet and ready to catch the murderer.

All I had to go on was the stuff everyone knew, and one other fact that no one knew but me. A thing I'd kept to myself so far. What Paul Price himself had told me how he wanted a bodyguard because he'd been finding things out, and how someone had tried to gouge his eye out.

Well, he hadn't lost his eye, but he'd got the head it came in smashed. Smashed to such a pulp the eye would never be much good to him again.

Who had done it?

A lot of people hadn't liked Paul Price. Letting my mind wander over the case, I could understand why. He'd played around with blackmail. He had Anderson under his thumb . . . Dolores Despana . . . the kid Winifred . . . Mrs Chip-Ebberly . . . maybe others. He was working a racket. He was out for dough. Dough and power. Yes. Price was a rat.

Okay. He was a rat. But so what? All men are rats, if you come down to it. And, rat or not, for a little while he had been my friend. A spark of decency, generosity, had burst into sudden flame. He'd promised to write about me in his column. Which meant fame, fortune, glory.

Yeah. He was my friend. He'd been killed. And when I got the bastard that did it, I'd see to it he died slow: hard and slow. I'd tear his arms off and watch him bleed . . . or I'd hold him over the stem of the furnace in the engine-room . . . I'd sit down and watch him die, and I'd love every minute of it.

Foolish, maybe. Call me a crazy, romantic crusader if you want. It's just that Paul Price was my friend, and that's the kind of guy I am.

Out of the corner of my eye I caught a movement in the murky, bewildering fog. I whirled. It was a steward, and he was trying to slink away unnoticed, but when I gave him a look he came cringing up like a dog.

'Yes, sir?' He stammered it out. I could see he was yellow. I showed him a five-spot.

'Where's that blonde tomato?' I asked him brusquely.

'Sir?' He gave me a stupid look.

I couldn't tell if his ignorance was genuine or not. 'That fluff. The blonde.'

'Sir?'

'You know who I mean. Dolores.'

'Miss Despana, sir?'

'Where is she?' I was getting tired of his stalling.

'Well, sir, I – I – I expect she's in her cabin, sir.'

I figured he was levelling. I flipped his pay into his face. It fluttered down, and he scrambled for it. As he reached for it I stepped on his hand and ground my heel on it, hard. There was a grinding, cracking sound. The steward was yellow, all right – he let out a shriek, and I laughed. I laughed again as he ran off holding on to one hand with the other.

It made me feel a little better, but not much. There was still a tight, hot feeling in my guts and it was like a big, heavy ball of molten lead and I knew it would be there till I had solved the crime.

I decided to go see Dolores. Oddly enough, I hadn't met her yet. I'd seen her and she'd seen me; and of course like the other dames on the ship she'd given me looks which I knew how to interpret, but we hadn't got together yet. But now the time had come. As I figured the angles, she might know something about Price that would help me.

The steward hadn't lied. She was in her cabin. Facing the door, her hands on her hips, smiling at me in challenge. Her hair was like yellow neon light, and her eyes were like violets, and she had full pouting red lips, but from the face down she was even better. You could tell because her black dress was like a coat of glossy paint. A *thin* coat.

'I've been expecting you, Spike,' she said. Her voice was low and throaty.

I found it hard to breathe. I pulled a packet of butts from my pocket, stuck one into my mouth and lit it, and threw another one in her direction. Watching her light it, I got myself under control.

'I've got a question to ask you, baby,' I told her.

'Ask all the questions you want, Spike,' she said. The violet eyes told me what questions she was hoping for, and what answer she would give. It nearly sidetracked me, but I jerked myself back to the business at hand.

'About Paul Price,' I said.

A curious expression flitted across her face. Suddenly her mouth and her eyes looked harder. I remembered how she'd made a play for Price. She was for sale – and her own price went down in my mind, like a toboggan slide. A moment ago I'd set her at two million bucks. Now she was worth maybe only a hundred grand.

'You saw a lot of him,' I went on.

'So what?' She blew out a defiant cloud of smoke.

'So that's your business. You're a grown-up girl, chicken. Unless it was you that bumped him off, and then it's very much my business. What I want to know right now is, did he ever say anything to you about having been attacked? About someone trying to gouge his eye out?'

'To – ' She stared at me. 'No, Spike! No! Never. Why?'

'Because someone did try. He mentioned it to me but he didn't say who did it, and I was too dumb to ask.' I felt screaming mad as I thought how easily I could have found out then – if I'd only known I would never see Price again! 'It stands to reason,' I went on. 'The guy who pulled a knife on him then is the one who got him eventually with a blackjack.'

Dolores stiffened. The violet eyes narrowed to slits. 'He never mentioned it to me, but I can guess who it was, Spike! It must have been the same person who attacked *me!*'

'Mrs Chip-Ebberly?' I'd heard about what happened at the boat-drill from the First Officer.

'Sure-' Dolores quivered. You could see the quiver travel all the way. . . . 'She tried to kill me! Why, my leg is all bruised from falling down that ladder – see!'

She hitched up the black silk skirt so I could see, inch by inch. How could I concentrate? I went over and pulled it down. I kissed her – then pushed her away.

'Yeah,' I said, trying to think about Mrs Chip-Ebberly. 'I want to have a little chat with that dame!'

'She's the killer, Spike! They say she's a smuggler, too – dope! She's in a dope-ring! And Paul Price found her out. She must be the killer!'

'Unless *you* are,' I said. I watched her reaction.

She opened the eyes wide and aimed them right at me. She put her arms around my neck clingingly and kissed me again. This time it was harder to push her away. She whispered: 'And if it was me that did it, Spike?'

'If it was you, baby,' I told her, 'it won't matter how swell your curves are. I'll beat you till you're black and green all over, and then I'll put a slug through your beautiful stomach.'

She shuddered. 'Well, it *wasn't* me!' She looked at me earnestly. 'Why, Paul was going to run a plug about me in his column. He was taking me up . . . it would have meant the big time. *Really* big time, Spike. Lights – Broadway – chincillas, instead of my crumby minks! . . . I have everything to lose by his murder. First my plug got stolen, and now people are saying it won't get printed because Paul is dead.' Her eyes filled with tears. She dashed them away.

I felt a lump in my throat. 'I know. I know how you feel. *He promised to write a plug for me, too.*' I stopped. The words were like red-hot coals struggling to find their way up from my guts. It was something I hadn't told a living soul so far. '*The plug never even got written. Some bastard killed him first.*'

Dolores looked at me. The hardness was gone from her eyes and mouth. 'Gee, Spike,' she whispered. Her voice was like honey. 'Gee . . . that's rough. Worse than with me, even. At least, mine got written.'

'Oh, I'll get by.' I gave her a lopsided grin.

Her voice changed. 'I wish I could do something to console you, Spike.' She smiled gaily as she tore off her dress with a silky ripping sound. Her eyes were purple flames.

'Oh, Spike,' she whispered. 'Am I being brazen?'

'You're just right,' I told her. 'I don't like women who are too reserved. Only, now, I've got some business . . .' I pushed her away. 'Just wait, Dolores, just wait!'

Outside the door I opened my notebook and put her name on my list. There weren't too many ahead of her. The redhead on B-deck. The stewardess down the line. The bleached blonde with the . . . On second thought, I crossed the bleached blonde off. That brought Dolores up a peg.

I could hardly wait.

Then I saw the old battle-axe, Mrs Chip-Ebberly, bearing down in my direction, with her layers of blankets and her knitting. I stopped where I was, shook out a butt and lit it, and waited till she came up. Then I stepped in front of her to block her way.

'I want a word with you,' I said.

The look she gave me would have congealed a blast-furnace. She said, 'I don't believe I know you.'

But I could be just as nasty as she could. Instead of moving like she obviously expected me to do, I just stood there and stretched out an arm to the opposite wall of the passage so as to bar her way.

'I'll introduce myself. The name's Spike Bludgeon. Occupation, private eye.'

She tried to duck past. I pushed her back and gave her a faceful of cigarette smoke. 'Not so fast,' I told her brusquely.

There was a wild look from the midst of her coughing and choking. She didn't get it. Nobody spoke to her like that. I figured it would be a good lesson in democracy for her.

'Just because you're royalty, don't think you can get away with anything you like,' I told her. 'A crook's a crook in my language.'

'Because I am *what?*'

I reached out and grabbed her knitting-bag. She let out a yowl. I pulled one of the needles out of whatever it was she was dreaming up. It was a long, shining, steel thing with a perfect tapering point. I threw the bag into a corner, and waved the needle in her face.

She was gibbering.

'Don't lose your shirt,' I told her. 'Take a look at this. . . . You used your ball of wool for an ulterior purpose. And maybe this needle too. It's just about right for sticking someone in the eye, isn't it?'

I looked at her hard, but I couldn't tell if her bewilderment was real or phony.

'Someone tried to gouge Paul Price's eye out,' I said softly. 'You wouldn't know a thing about that, would you?'

She just looked at me, speechless, her jaw hanging down. Her refusal to cooperate was making me lose my temper. I took her by the arm. '*Would* you?' I spat the words out.

'No!' It came in a bubbling gasp.

I tossed the needle away. 'Okay, grandma,' I said quietly. 'Maybe I believe you and maybe I don't. We'll let it go for now. Just remember, a crook is open to suspicion. . . . I know about your smuggling game. Just remember I got my eye on you. Don't go pushing people downstairs any more. Especially blondes . . . I got my own use for them.'

I watched her react, gave her a harsh laugh, and strolled away.

Back in the Lounge there was a hush when I entered. There was a quality in the air. I could feel it. . . . Hostility . . . thick, cold. With dirty fear mixed in somewhere. I let my eye run over the passengers slowly. I saw their furtive glances. I could tell they were avoiding my eye. There was only one thing that could mean – *guilt*. There was some guilty knowledge. they were hiding from me.

Just thinking about it I got so mad the sweat rolled down my forehead and my back. I picked up an ash-tray and hurled it against the wall. I went out, and met the First Officer. He said he had been hunting for me.

'Are there any developments, Mr Bludgeon?' he asked.

'I don't know.' I was still keeping my one secret fact to myself. 'I wish I knew more about those business deals Price had on.'

'Do you think he was killed for money?'

'What do *you* think?' I looked at him sharply. He didn't answer right away, and I had to repeat the question. I said, 'What do *you* think?'

'Oh.' There was a strange look on his face. 'I didn't know, I thought there might be other reasons why people might kill. I mean . . . Well, there's love, maybe, or being jealous, or people kill for the sake of an idea sometimes . . .'

'Love, maybe. Yeah,' I said. 'But murder for an *idea?* Bugs, no.'

'But if it was – ' He licked his lips. 'Well, you're the expert, Mr Bludgeon. I haven't had much experience of this sort of thing.' He sounded nervous. I couldn't tell why.

I said bitterly: 'That's right. . . . I'm the expert. And if you're smart you'll never try to be one. You'll stay away from crimes. Stay on your little ship, out in the middle of the ocean, and perhaps you'll have a stray killing or two but you'll never see the things I see. The rackets, the corruption, the filth . . .'

He looked like a kid whose ice-cream cone has been stolen by a big boy. 'I always thought a private investigator had an exciting, adventurous life – romantic, so to speak.'

'Bugs,' I repeated. I decided I would tell him about the attack on Price. 'I'd like to speak to you – privately,' I said. 'Maybe there *has* been a development.'

'We can be quiet in here.' He led me to the cabin that was being used as headquarters.

We found the Doctor in there. He jumped when he saw us.

'I've lost a page of my manuscript.' His pudgy face cracked

137

with worry. 'I thought I might have left it in. – Ah!' The worry uncracked. 'Here it is!'

I looked over his shoulder at the paper he'd picked up from under a table. He seemed to be telling the truth. You could see it was poetry because the right-hand margin was uneven.

The way he cheered up when he'd got it back, you'd have thought it was something important. He began to talk, very briskly. 'Waggish here has been telling me about the investigation,' he said, 'and the various techniques you chaps use. How Sir Jon. Nappleby uses books, and Mr Poireau likes things to be tidy, and you say it's good manners that count the most in being a detective – '

The First Officer got all red in the face. He said quickly, 'No, no, that's someone else you're thinking of.' He looked at me apologetically, and I could see he hadn't really meant any harm. 'What *do* you consider most important in being a detective, Mr Bludgeon?'

I gave them both a hard smile. 'Guts,' I told him. 'Guts are what make the difference. If you've got guts you get the killer. If you haven't you get bumped off yourself.'

The Doctor nodded, interrupting me. 'Like Mr Price,' he said. 'He wasn't a brave man and he got killed.'

The First Officer looked at him in surprise. 'How do you mean, he wasn't brave? Do you mean because he got seasick?'

'Well, that; he came to me for pills. But after that he came again.' The Doctor sounded vague. The First Officer was frowning a little, staring at him. 'He got some soot in his eye from the smokestack, and came running to me for me to get it out. Well, when I went after the soot he yelled out and began to jump up and down and acted as if I was trying to hurt him.'

It didn't take me long to get it. I went cold all over. Before I even knew how screaming, scarlet-mad I was, I was on my feet and I'd slashed out at the sawbones with a quick right that had him staggering against the wall. He didn't have time to take in what had happened before I got hold of his arm and was twisting it up behind his back till the bones were ready to break.

The First Officer shouted, 'What the devil?' but I paid no attention.

'Go on – talk!' I ordered the Doctor. The words came hissing out like live steam.

He gurgled something.

'Talk!' I twisted the arm some more, digging my fingers deep.

'But – but what do you want me to say?' His fat face was as white as the belly of a dead fish.

I was impatient. I whipped out my .45 and put it to his head.

The First Officer grabbed my arm. At the same moment the Doctor's eyes rolled up so the whites showed, and he fell down in a heap. I had my foot up ready to kick his ribs in when the First Officer shook my arm harder. I wheeled impatiently. 'What is it?'

'You're – you're making a mistake!' he said.

'I don't like people to say that to me.' My voice was like a shower of winter hail.

He got pale, but he had guts, all right. He argued with me, even though he couldn't help stuttering. 'I'm not – not – a detective, Mr Bludgeon,' he said, and then he stopped and swallowed. His eyes were fixed on my gun. 'I don't know what clue you've found out. But – why did you go for the Doctor?'

I explained about the attack on Price.

'But the Doctor wouldn't try to gouge an eye out! No matter what Price thought. If he was getting a cinder out, perhaps, his hand slipped, or something or that sort. It must have been an accident!'

'Accident!' I pulled out a crumpled butt and lit it. After a drag on it I felt a little better. 'There's no such thing as accident, in my experience, Waggish. Murder – yes. Assault – yes. Suicide – yes, sometimes. Accidents, no.'

'But *why* would he do a thing like that?'

I shrugged. 'Why? That'll come out in time. Meanwhile I just want to punish him for doing it.'

He looked down at the Doctor. 'Even so,' he said, 'he couldn't have done the *murder*, you know. It would have been a physical impossibility.'

Well, he hadn't convinced me. Not a bit. But the fact that the Doctor has been somewhere else when the murder took place would have to be taken into account, maybe. I decided to let the First Officer have his way for a while. The Doctor was still out. I tapped his head with the butt of my .45 to make sure he would stay that way for a good long time, so he couldn't do any harm.

'Okay,' I said. 'I'll talk to him again tomorrow.'

I went to see Dolores again.

'I'm still waiting, Spike,' she said.

'That's the girl.' I kissed her – then pushed her away, hating to do it. Her face wasn't hard any longer, and her price had gone up.

'You're so wonderful, Spike,' she muttered. 'All those ugly scars . . . your broken nose . . . and the ear that's chopped off. . . . How could they do it, Spike? How could anyone bear to hurt you?'

'The ones who did it are dead,' I told her. 'People who cross me usually end up that way.'

She gave a violent shudder. 'Do you think the killer will be caught, Spike?'

'He's bound to be. And I hope it's me that gets him . . . You see, Dolores, the trouble is, if any of those other dicks catch him they'll turn him over to the First Officer. And while the First Officer may be okay in himself, he's like an honest cop on land – at the mercy of a system. He'd just have to turn the killer in and hold him for trial by jury. Whereas if *I* get him . . . well, he'll be sorry he did it.'

She shuddered again. 'I'm frightened, Spike!'

'Don't worry!' I gave a crooked grin. 'You're safe with me. And maybe – maybe we'll get that piece about you into the papers yet!'

'Oh, Spike!' Her violet eyes were misty. She didn't say anything else, but she looked at me the way you look at the altar in church. Then she was clinging to me and kissing me, and this time I couldn't push her away. . . .

And that's why I was still a little dizzy next morning, too dizzy to use my head and go after the Doctor first thing. Instead I went off at a tangent. I told the First Officer there was another possibility besides dough and love, as murder motives. I thought to myself it would explain the Doctor's motive too but I didn't say so.

'Crazy people will kill just because they're crazy,' I explained.

'Crazy people?'

'Yeah. People who are bats. Schizophrenics. Psychos. Sadists. Where normal people like you and me would need a motive, they don't.' I lit a cigarette. 'So that's why I want to see the Captain.'

The First Officer opened his eyes big. 'The Captain!'

'Yeah. He's supposed to be bugs, isn't he? Well, then, I just want to take a look at him. I want to see for myself. I can recognize crazy people . . . there's a certain look in their eyes.'

'But, I say – ' I gave him a frown, and he stopped arguing. 'I'll try to arrange it, Mr Bludgeon,' he said. His voice was shaky. I gave him a level look. Honest? Maybe, but he was the victim of a system, all right: the slave of a foolish hierarchy . . . afraid of superiors, of rules and regulations, of obsolete stupid traditions . . .

I didn't wait for him to arrange it. I went up to the bridge. The Captain was standing at the rail looking into the fog. When he heard me he turned around and I got a good look at his face. Yes, he was bugs. His eyes were greenish and glittery and mad, like haunted emeralds. I was starting to ask him something when he said, 'The bridge is not open to passengers. You will have to go below at once.'

I'd come all set to be friendly, but I couldn't take that, even from a lunatic. I said, 'I've seen all I came for,' but I knew he wouldn't get the point, so to make sure he remembered my visit I flipped my half-smoked butt into his face. It caught in his beard and as I wheeled and walked off I could smell singeing hair. I heard a bellow behind me as I went down – it took him that long to cotton on to the fact that someone had guts enough to treat him like an ordinary mortal. I gave a bitter laugh.

But after that I didn't feel like laughing. It was time to visit the Doctor again. I should have had a premonition . . . a tight, hot shrieking in my guts. I should have remembered what happens to the women who love me . . . the poor, fated chippies who come like lovely naked moths to a brilliant flame too searing for them to endure. I should have known.

When I opened the door I saw Dolores. She was lying on the settee. One beautiful arm hung down. And her face was covered with blood.

The Doctor was bending over her.

I couldn't even scream. Cold ran down my back and fire ran up into my brain. Before the Doctor had even swung about, hiding her from me, I had my gun out. There were footsteps along the passage outside, voices yelling. 'He went in there!' Then I knew I wouldn't have time to give him the nice, slow, crawling death he deserved. I gave him a slug in the guts, and as he staggered and fell down I was already whirling about. A whole line of uniforms came at me down the passage.

I was blind with a wild, ravaging fury – but I can aim and shoot by instinct. I knew I got one guy in the head, and one in the chest, and another in the guts. Then someone came up behind me and my head split apart with jagged pain and the deck hit my face with a vicious crash.

When I came to I ached all over. My head pounded agonizingly, and there was a scratch on the little finger of my left hand a full inch long. Broodingly I wondered if they provided Band-aid for prisoners in the *Florabunda*'s brig. I stared at the bars. Then as the whole thing welled up into my memory I hit my head against the wall in silent rage.

When I came to again the First Officer was looking in through the bars. 'I'm sorry about all this, Mr Bludgeon,' he said. 'But it was the captain's orders.'

I gave a bitter laugh. 'I suppose he doesn't like having his officers liquidated,' I said with a sneer. 'But at least I accounted for that rat who killed Dolores . . . and a few more guys besides.'

A queer look crossed his face. 'But – ' he said. He licked his lips nervously. 'But, Mr Bludgeon, Miss Despana wasn't killed!'

I leaped to my feet, ignoring the pain.

'She wasn't even hurt. It was only – she had a nosebleed, Mr Bludgeon, and she went to Doctor for treatment.'

The sweat rolled down my body. I couldn't speak.

'But don't worry,' he said. 'The Doctor isn't dead, either, or any of those other chaps.'

'What?' I knew now he was lying. My .45 has never missed. . . .

'No. I – I changed your bullets for blank cartridges whilst

142

you were taking a shower. I was afraid you might do something hasty, and then regret it afterwards.'

'*What?*'

'Aye. So I just came down. . . . I was afraid you'd have it
on your mind and I wanted to tell you not to worry. We'll
see about getting you out, but the Captain . . . You are really
safer here.' He gave me a stupid, anxious smile. 'Cheerio.'

I let out all the curse words I knew. At first I felt only sheer
blind fury. Then a nasty, crawling doubt crept in.

Why had Waggish *really* changed my bullets for blanks?

He knew I was out to get the killer, didn't he? The only
reason he could have for wanting to stop me from shooting
was – that he was the killer himself!

Or that he was sheltering the killer!

True, he had seemed honest. He had never met Price. He
was responsible for the murder's being investigated.

I thought it over. I struck the wall with my fists again and
again till the flesh was raw and bleeding.

I couldn't make up my mind.

But one thing I knew.

First, I'd get out of this place. And then, *I'd get the
murderer of Paul Price, if I had to kill everyone on board
the ship to do it!*

CHAPTER 11

MALLORY KING

Mallory King paced the deck. He stared out unhappily into the fog. He flipped a cigarette into a sandbox, jabbed a match against its folder, and lit another cigarette. He found himself humming:

> 'The farmer takes his wife,
> The farmer takes his wife,
> Heigh-ho, the derry-o,
> The farmer takes his wife.'

And paused in his harried perambulation to groan aloud. *The Farmer in the Dell!*

Very well, so he *could* operate only on the nursery level on this voyage! Shameful – but the whole case was befuddling. It had a tantalizing simplicity like 'The Farmer in the Dell', and made just about as much sense.

Heigh-ho, the derry-o, The farmer in the dell. The words began to jingle again. *The cat takes the rat, the rat takes the cheese . . .*

Mallory informed himself sardonically: *And Mallory King, the great detective, the master-mind of Manhattan, takes the cake!* All this time, and the murderer was still at large!

Still, the farmer and his bucolic adventures might lead somewhere. Nursery rhymes, after all, lie close to the heart of the racial experience. They suggest fundamental things – birth – death. They follow archetypal patterns of human life. They are basic.

To what archetype did the murder of Paul Price belong?

Mallory shook his head impatiently. He reviewed the case

144

in his mind for the trillionth time. He went over the list of exasperating questions he had formulated:

Why had the body been left aboard? Because the killer was too weak to heave it over the rail? That would mean a woman. Well: the female of the species. . . . On the other hand, it had taken strength to kill with a single blow.

Or because the killer wanted Price to be found – in order, say, to obviate legal doubt of his death? That would mean Winifred: little Winifred with her dark eyes and her kittenlike innocence. Mallory mumbled 'No!' aloud, and a passenger standing near him flinched in alarm. Vaguely, Mallory apologized. It wasn't mere sentimentality that made him reluctant to view Winifred as the murderer, surely?

Or there might be another reason for wanting the body found – a reason linked with that curious decoration found underneath it; which led to question number two: *What was meant by the scarf and the pipe?* Was it Price who had had them, or his murderer? The pipe was brand-new; the scarf belonged to an innocent boy. Why had they – if they had – been left deliberately on the scene?

Why had the cosh been kept, and then used in a too-crude, too-obvious frame against Homer T. Anderson? Again, Mallory mentally kicked himself. If only he had kept his eyes open – The murder weapon obtained under his very nose! Mallory tugged hard at his unoffending hair, and was mortified in spirit.

Why had Anderson's cheque been used in the same obvious, crude, and leaky frame? Who had tried to compromise him? Was he clever enough to frame himself? And if so, why? The frame had made no real difference one way or the other. And Mallory was sure that Anderson, at least, had not picked up the blackjack that night.

Why had a sheet of paper been removed from Price's type-writer and then thrust under the noses of the detectives? And why, oh, why, had the killer perpetrated that idiotic, that cretinous, that infuriating twaddle at the bottom of the paper? Mallory stared at his copy:

'Well I find there is another master-mind on board who is a horse of a different colour. He is a specialist in murder too but from another angle and he is having fun and games whilst the Sherlocks sleep. He does not know I have found him out

but next time we meet FIREWORKS MAY BE EXPECTED. THE
REAL NAME OF THIS CROOK IS NOT ON HIS PASSPORT IT IS
GIB.'

As Trajan Beare had seen at once, it betrayed the work of
an Englishman. Yet . . . Whoever had written it, it was an
insult to the intelligence. Who could be expected to believe
that Price had written it? Who did the killer think he was
dealing with, anyway? Or did he *want* it to look like
nonsense?

*Had Mrs Chip-Ebberly really tried to kill Dolores Despana
by pushing her down the companionway?* If the answer was
yes, she was presumably the killer. But would she, could she
have perpetrated that gibberish? Or left a red and yellow
scarf and a pipe behind?

If the answer was 'No', either Dolores had lied or she was
mistaken. Mallory guessed she was not above a lie; but this
lie would make her a better actress than the critics thought.
So good in fact that she needn't be pursuing Anderson in the
hopes of a subsidy. If, on the other hand, she was honestly
mistaken, the whole episode meant exactly nothing.

Mallory had talked with Mrs Chip-Ebberly. He knew she
lived in a private, moribund world, archaic, obsolete. She
disapproved of him as of everyone else on the ship. She froze
him with her glances. He would creep trembling from a
session with her and, as he slowly thawed, would find himself
still uncertain whether she was guilty. Her smuggling, and
her delusions of espionage as in a Hitchcock movie, did
nothing to clarify the issue.

Mallory had talked with Anderson, too, and with Win
Price, and with the Doctor and the Purser and the First
Officer. And with anyone else he could find to talk to. The
result was *nil*.

He had talked with them all – with the persons who were,
by the evidence of his senses and his logic, the suspects. And
Winifred Price was young and worried and eager to help, and
full of screwy psychological theories that led nowhere, and
Anderson was crass and stupid and bursting with awareness
of his wealth and importance, and the others were what they
were, each in his own natural kind, species, and genus. And
the Doctor, the Purser, and the First Officer had alibis which
were good enough, and they had had no reason to kill Price.

Or so it seemed – for Mallory was a cautious soul and would not let his liking (for he liked them all) interfere with his detection.

He had given due thought to the Purser's infatuation with Win. But when he opened a discussion of it with the First Officer, Mr Waggish had only looked blank, and agreed readily enough that the Purser was 'in love with the lass'.

'Then – ' Mallory sought a tactful way of suggesting that this provided one of the more commonplace murder motives. 'If he wants to marry her, and knew the uncle would object – '

Mr Waggish interrupted him. 'Surely to goodness – You detectives keep saying that. You don't really think he *would?*'

'Kill Price?'

'Marry Miss Price!'

'But if he's in *love* with the wench?' Mallory argued reasonably.

Mr Waggish was honestly puzzled and shook his head. 'Tom's in love on *every* voyage,' he explained.

'On every – You mean he goes about wearing that dying-cow expression for some girl on *every* trip?'

'That's it,' the First Officer said simply as Mallory groaned. 'You might call it his idiosyncrasy. Sometimes it's a nice young lady like Miss Price, sometimes it's – well, a different type. No one thinks anything of it.'

'I see. And – er – his fiancée back home?'

'Of course he's in love with her too,' said the First Officer matter-of-factly. 'Between trips.'

'I see,' said Mallory again. A new thought came to him. 'What would happen', he asked interestedly, 'if a time came when there were no girls aboard? If all the female passengers were of the Chip-Ebberly vintage?'

'I never thought.' The First Officer was equally struck with the idea, and a far-away look came into his eyes. 'I wonder', he murmured, 'if it could be arranged.'

Mallory left him to his speculations, and returned to his own.

He had scoured the *Florabunda*. He had even, in the wake of Sir Jon. Nappleby and Spike Bludgeon, braved the Captain in his cabin. Who had visions of deep-sea Edens and thought good sailors turned into mermen when they died.

Who acted like a cross between Herman Melville's Captain Ahab and the god Poseidon.

Who had been nowhere in the offing when the cosh was stolen.

Who had been happy to hear of Price's demise, but had — it had been determined — an adamantine alibi for the time when it occurred.

Who had refused to say a word to Mallory King and had been almost ready to order him thrown overboard for approaching him; only the First Officer had come to the rescue.

Meanwhile, tension mounted. No one enjoys knowing that a killer is roaming about unchecked, especially when there is no way of removing oneself from his neighbourhood short of lowering a lifeboat.

Mallory lit another cigarette and withdrew into intensive contemplation. He dug into his own recollections of Price; things his father and other police officials had told him. But these memories only reinforced his opinion that Price had been a rat. A character in search of a murderer. A nuisance to the forces of law and order and decency all his life; libel, extortion, tax evasion, and finally (in a passive and involuntary way to be sure) homicide.

Or rather, Mallory thought bitterly, rodenticide.

He stiffened. Something stirred in the depths of his mind. Rodenticide. The killing of a rodent. The death of a rat . . . But the thought slid away uselessly.

When Mr Waggish approached him, Mallory threw up his hands. 'Don't ask me,' he warned. 'No, I have *not* found your criminal. I begin to think the whole thing is hallucination.'

Mr Waggish, who was literal-minded, looked at him uncertainly. 'But surely it was a real murder? And we've got to get the killer!'

'Well — there's a little time left. We may find the answer.'

'We had better,' said the First Officer. 'The Old Man is getting impatient. Sooner than be held up in port, he'll pick on some victim at random, charge him with the murder, and sail off home.'

'Probably he'll pick one of us detectives,' Mallory groaned.

'It would just as likely be me,' Mr Waggish pointed out. 'Since he thinks I ought to have settled the matter by now.

And, while I'd enjoy a bit of time in New York, I'd as lief not spend it in quod. So I wish we'd catch the real killer.'

Mallory demanded: 'And what do you suppose my father will say if we dock without my being able to point to the killer? And the newspapers! We'll be the laughing-stock of two continents. Think of the headlines. We'll be a modern *Narrenschiff*, or Ship of Fools. If I could *only* discover the pattern.'

'The *pattern*!' exclaimed the First Officer.

'My cases', Mallory explained, 'always have some underlying pattern; some theme, some *motif* which unites and gives meaning to details which, on the surface, seem merely arbitrary and fantastic.'

The First Officer nodded intelligently.

'For instance, in one case the killer used the concept of the chain of evolution, working up from the murder of frogs, and dogs, and so on, to Man. Another, with an Old Testament complex, used the scheme of the Ten Commandments. This time – '

'Yes?' Mr Waggish asked eagerly.

'This time – Darn it,' Mallory said plaintively, 'I simply don't know. The details remain fantastic, like that scarf and pipe. *Obscurum per obscurius*.'

'It's odd,' Mr Waggish agreed. 'The way they just lay there, the pipe all tangled up in the scarf.' He said hopefully, 'But perhaps they just happened to be there? It might have *nothing to do* with the murder!'

'They don't make sense,' Mallory told him absently, 'whatever tune they were meant to pipe.'

Pipe! *Pipe!*

Mallory gasped. He gulped. 'Quick,' he cried. 'Where can I find a copy of Browning's poems?'

'What?'

A picture formed itself in Mallory's mind. Brooks. Papers. A copy of Browning. Papers . . . 'The Doctor's office!' he exclaimed.

'If you want poetry, that is where it would most likely be. But why?' Mr Waggish asked, looking vaguely unhappy.

'I'll tell you after I've checked this hunch,' Mallory told him. 'This may be what I've been waiting for – the clue to the labyrinth – the Figure in the Carpet! I've got to see the Doctor. I want to borrow a book.'

Al Mallory's greeting the Doctor grunted without even looking up from the desk where he was writing away furiously with a scratchy pen and trying to keep his papers from sliding about too much. He was pale, and there were bits of sticking-plaster and bandaging on his face and neck, the aftermath of his encounter with the impetuous Spike Bludgeon. He looked up as Mallory leaned over him to pull the Browning from the shelf.

'Ha, Mr King! Sit down. If you want poetry, why read that old stuff? Let me read you a bit of this!' Holding up a sheet of his manuscript, he read aloud ebulliently:

'Her champions, though victorious, suffered fatal wounds
    enow:
Gazella wept on hearing their grand ultimate miaow.
"O Leo, King, who reign'st on high in majesty Zodiacal,
Regard thy kin! Avenge their death!" (she cried in woe
    cardiacal),
"And for my part I will erect on this ill-fated site
A golden tomb, and mourn their loss with tears and decent
    feline rite." '

'Superb!' Mallory said earnestly, his hand on the doorknob.
    'But that's only the beginning!'
Mallory pleaded a pressing engagement. He fled.
In his cabin he leafed through Browning with trembling fingers. The story of the Pied Piper of Hamelin came back from his childhood: the plague of rats – the concern of the town councillors – the mysterious stranger who offered, for a consideration, to rid them of the pests, and lured the rats after him with his enchanting music into the River Weser, where they drowned. But where was that passage . . . Surely he remembered, in the description of that quaint remorseless figure, the Piper, that tall thin man in particoloured coat – Yes!

                                        round his neck
    A scarf of red and yellow stripe,

150

To match with his coat of self-same cheque;
AND AT THE SCARF'S END HUNG A PIPE

Mallory smacked the page with his open palm triumphantly.

The meaning of the scarf and pipe found under Price's body was incontrovertible. *They were symbols* – the pipe in a punning way. *The murder was symbolic!*

Everyone who had met Paul Price, or even *seen* him merely, had instinctively compared him to a rat. And the killer was deliberately identifying himself with the Pied Piper – the *slayer of rats!*

When he could control his excitement enough to talk, Mallory expounded his discovery to the First Officer. The First Officer was thrilled and delighted.

Mallory forestalled his inevitable question. 'I still don't know who did it! But now we know something about the character of the killer! . . . I've got to think.'

Looking in, hours later, Mr Waggish found him surrounded by sheets of paper, scribbled over cabbalistically. He saw: WINIFRED INIWDREF DOLORES SLODORE EORSODL EBBERLYPICH . . .

Mallory grinned at him. 'I haven't gone crazy. At least I don't think so. I'm just working on the suspects' names anagrammatically.'

'I see . . .'

But Mallory, out of kindness, explained: 'I mean, I rearrange the letters. . . . Often names provide vital clues, you know. They can influence character. In one of my cases there were two brothers, called Kane and Judah: *their real names were Cain and Judas!*'

Alone again, he worked on patiently.

PAUL PRICE.

Paul Pry. Paul Pry. Pied Piper.

Paul Price, the quintessential quidnunc.

No, that meant nothing. Only that one got nowhere by minding one's p's and q's.

P . . . Q . . . R . . . Rats. The Pied Piper chased rats. So did terriers. So did ferrets. So did – most obviously – cats.

Mallory let his mind wander. It strayed back to that garbled piece of pseudo-Price:

THE REAL NAME OF THIS CROOK IS NOT ON HIS PASSPORT IT IS GIB.

Now why should he think that gibberish?

Gib – gibberish – GIB! *GIB!*

Something clicked in Mallory's mind, and this time it did not escape. He whirled around and grabbed his dictionary from the bunk, where he had flung it in the course of his anagrammatizing. Gib . . . Yes!

'gib. (Abbr. fr. Gilbert, name of a cat) A familiar name for a cat. Hence, a cat, esp. a tomcat.'

The last word in that forged paragraph was not the first syllable of 'gibberish'. It *was the complete name itself. Gib!*

Mallory's head spun. For that was not all. . . . Gib, he realized, is not the most common type-name for a cat. Rather, the traditional name is . . . Desperately he tried to remember animal names. There was Reynard the Fox and Chanticleer the Cock and Gilbert the Cat, whence Gib, and the White Cat and Puss in Boots. Cats are Grimalkin or Greymalkin or Tabby or . . .

Mallory remembered *Romeo and Juliet*. Who was that swaggering bully whom Mercutio called the 'king of cats' because he had a cat's name? King of cats – ah! Mercutio had challanged him to a duel. He had said: 'Tybalt, you rat-catcher, will you walk?'

Tybalt! Tybalt the cat! *T!*

Mallory felt an electric shock go through him. He jumped up and grabbed his jacket. He found the First Officer, and demanded the passports of the suspects, or their Customs forms, or anything with their names in full. Mr Waggish sent the request on to the Purser. Mallory bit his thumb. At length the Purser came in with an inquisitive look at him and a request that the forms be returned to his office.

Mallory flipped through them impatiently. Mrs Chip-Ebberly – her name was Arabella Felicia Sophia. Price, Winifred; Price, Paul – Anderson, Anderson – Anderson, Homer THEOBALD!

Mallory cried in exultation: 'Theobald!'

'Theobald?' Mr Waggish repeated dazedly.

'Theobald', Mallory explained, 'is the very same name as

Tybalt. Another spelling, that's all; like Tibbald. They all used to be pronounced the same. And Tybalt is the *Cat!* The cat of cats – the immortal, dedicated enemy of rats!

'The killer, who left the scarf and pipe to show he was a rat-exterminator like the Pied Piper, also wrote cryptically, in a passage purporting to be written by Price but actually describing *himself*, of a monster criminal called *Gib*. Now Gib, like Tybalt, means Cat! (And note that GIB spelled backwards is BIG!)

'In other words, the killer is a clever, devious, diabolical fanatic, rash and brilliant, who, with the inevitable conceit of the murderer, *thinks of himself as a super-cat!*'

The First Officer sat down abruptly. He was awestruck. 'But – ' he stammered feebly.

Mallory, intoxicated, asked: 'What?'

'But it doesn't make *sense*, Mr King!'

'It makes its own special, sinister, fateful sense! The murderer is working symbolically. In his own warped way, he loves to play with what is clearly a better than average fund of philological information!'

'But – Anderson?'

'I know,' Mallory granted. 'He's not the type I've just described, or doesn't seem so. And it may be that someone is trying to build a frame against him on the fact that he happens to have the mystic name of Theobald. But don't you see? We've assumed that the killer is a rather bungling, clumsy worker. No careful normal killer would be so careless and untidy. But once hypothesize that the killer is abnormal – a Machiavellian genuis – and see what happens! We must recast our whole interpretation. What formerly seemed stupidity must be deliberate pretence of stupidity. That spelling, for instance: "colour" and the use of "whilst" – the killer need not be British. He may be an American who has adopted English usage to focus suspicion on one of you Britishers. He may even be quite strong enough to have thrown Price overboard, but chosen to leave him on display with the pipe and scarf as a triumphant symbol of his achievement and a challenging hint to his own identity! He may be clever enough to mask as a stupid – as stupid Homer T. Anderson! After all, don't forget the Kiddie *Kit!* Let's pay a little visit to that gentleman.'

153

As they went down the passage Mallory said more soberly: 'Darn it. I forgot. I suppose he'll want his lawyer on hand.'

Mr Waggish said happily: 'He'll not have his wish, then, Mr King. Mr Pason has sacked him as a client – he had too much of him.'

Mallory grinned, and knocked.

Anderson gave them a sullen and suspicious glare from his small three-cornered eyes. There were traces of a heavy scent in his cabin, and Mallory guessed it was not long since Miss Despana had paid a call.

Mallory said suavely, 'We'd like to ask you just one question.'

'You mean you master-minds haven't caught the killer yet?' Anderson spoke with mastodontal irony. 'Well, I've told you all everything I know – over and over again. What's the sense of questions? All you do is talk. You don't seem to get anywhere at all.'

Contempt brought expressiveness to his stolid face, a gleam of some kind – a kind of ersatz intelligence, Mallory thought. *Or was it more genuine?*

Mallory demanded sharply: 'What is your middle name?'

Anderson's mouth fell open. He hesitated. Then: 'Theobald. So what?'

'Exactly. Well, Mr Homer Theobald Anderson, it may interest you to know that we are looking for a cat!'

Mallory watched him narrowly for a reaction. He got it. With a vengeance!

The triangular face went putty-coloured, then purple. He jumped up. 'My God!' he ejaculated thickly. 'My God! I think everyone on this damn ship is crazy! I – I a *cat!* I – my God, a killer, and you talk about looking for a cat! I – I think I must be getting a nervous breakdown.'

He sat down with an ungraceful bump and said preposterously: 'I wish I was home in New York.'

He began to sob.

The First Officer looked away, red with embarrassment and cleared his throat. Mallory regarded the display coldly. Was it fright? nerves? Or was it cunning – consummate histrionic skill? Genuine? Imitation?

Whichever it was, Anderson had more resilience than Mallory had thought. His fit ended quickly. He pulled himself together and demanded: 'What is all this crap about cats, anyway?'

'You're sure it means nothing to you? Cats? *Rats*, Mr Anderson?'

Anderson said disgustedly: 'Naturally I know what cats are. We even make them – but that's the animal department, and I don't have anything to do with it. I'm not interested in animals, only in bombs – ' A new vigour came to him at the thought of his darling death-rays. He pointed a thick, accusing finger at Mr Waggish. 'If you're looking for the crook, look at him! He took my toys away. Or look at that so-called Doctor!'

'It's no use throwing names around,' said Mallory. Machiavel or moron, Anderson was thoroughly objectionable, he decided. 'People don't kill without a motive, you know.'

'I told you before, he had a motive. Price insulted him. He said his poetry stank.'

Mallory sensed that the First Officer had stiffened slightly. Avoiding his eye, he told Anderson coldly: 'You mean, I suppose, that you told Mr Beare that you overheard Price call the Doctor incompetent? We have naturally assumed that he was disparaging his competence as *physician*.'

'What difference does it make? I just forgot – but I heard him say something about poetry, too. And do you want to know how I happened to hear? I – '

'Don't tell us,' Mallory said wearily. 'You were in the apple-barrel.'

'What?'

'It's in a book,' Mallory told him. 'Boys used to read it before you gave them atom-rays to play with.'

As he went out with the First Officer, they met Dolores Despana. She gave them a breath-taking smile, and passed Anderson's door as if she had no idea where it led to.

'What do you think, Mr King?' asked the First Officer. 'He doesn't act like a super-cat to *me*, somehow – '

Mallory sighed. 'I know. But remember, our killer is a superlatively clever actor. At least Anderson gave us one useful item.'

Mr Waggish blurted out, 'If you mean his saying Price insulted the Doctor, why everyone agrees the Doctor wouldn't murder for that!'

155

Mallory said mildly, 'We all have agreed that the Doctor takes his professional responsibilities – er – lightly. But animadversions on his epic would be something else again.'

'He wouldn't kill on any account. I'm positive! And he surely does not think he is a *Cat!*'

Mallory smiled at his troubled lean face. 'Don't worry too much about it. And of course, I may be wrong about all this. I'm always making mistakes.'

The First Officer looked at him. 'Mistakes?' He said rather shyly: 'I can't believe that of you, Mr King. I think your, your *theorizing* is brilliant! And the things you know! It's as if – as if you had an encyclopaedia in your cabin, and a book of quotations!'

Taken aback, Mallory nearly blushed. 'O Watson, Watson, thy name is Waggish!' he declaimed. 'You should talk to my father, and you'd hear about my errors!'

But he felt absurdly touched and flattered by the sincerity of this admiration. He had to tell himself severely that he must not allow himself to bask in it. The case was anything but solved.

The Doctor was still scribbling away when Mallory returned the Browning, but this time he looked up promptly. 'Was it any help?'

'It was, thanks.' Mallory added: 'I seem to be in a mood for poetry Doctor. I wonder if you'd permit me to look at *your* opus?'

The Doctor's face shone with unbelieving pleasure. 'Delighted!' he cried. He began to fumble through his manuscript. 'I'll read it to you now!'

Mallory told him quickly: 'I always have to see a thing to appreciate it. I was struck by some lines you recited to me earlier. Could I have a look at that part?'

The Doctor bent to find the page. Casually, Mallory asked: 'Why was Price so objectionable about your poem?'

'Him!' the Doctor muttered, still rummaging about. 'Ah, this must be the passage you want.'

'It must be hard', Mallory insinuated sympathetically, 'having rude things said.'

Straightening up, the Doctor looked at him with an unexpected glint in his eye. 'Price was damned uncivil, aye. Why, he said I couldn't even rhyme "cat" and "rat"! *Me!* He gave a short laugh, and went on with a sudden change of tone: 'But why should I care, Mr King, since he had never read a single word of "Tipptoppus and Gazella"? Or any other epic, I expect. He was a thorough boor. Now if *you*, after reading this, were to belittle my ability – ' A complacent smile dismissed such an eventuality as too silly for consideration.

'He hadn't read any of it, you say?'

The Doctor's smile became a little strained. 'Did I no' tell you that he said I couldn't rhyme?'

Mallory apologized hastily, and the Doctor went on, soothed: 'You'd be amazed how difficult it is to find people who appreciate such works, nevertheless. They have time for newspapers, or thrillers, or the B.B.C., or – or making love; but for heroic poetry, no!'

'Thanks.' Mallory reached over for the pages the Doctor held. 'I promise to take good care of it.'

The Doctor started. 'You want to take it away?'

'I'll be careful,' Mallory said firmly.

'But – ' The Doctor frowned a little.

'Thanks.'

'Aye – 'tis my only copy,' the Doctor admonished him, following him to the door. 'And I don't know that passage by heart at all – '

Mallory went back to his cabin. He took off his jacket, then his shoes. He read through the Doctor's *magnum opus*, or rather that infinitesimal fraction of it which had been so reluctantly surrendered to his charge. From what he could make out, the heroine had at this stage of her career been rescued from a Fate Worse Than Death by an army of noble lions who gave up their lives in her defence.

O Leo, King, who reign'st on high in majesty Zodiacal . . .

Mallory put the pages neatly into his table drawer.

The pile of cigarette stubs grew.

He sent for coffee.

He let his meals go by.

He paced the floor.

His mind whirled.

A fanatic. A super-cat. A rat-killer. Pipers and cats.

Cats – lions – Leo.

He must not read too much into it, he reminded himself. Such episodes were partly a matter of convention. Epic convention.

Conventions. . . . *There were conventions of another kind, too!*

Mallory shivered. He remembered another Cat. He saw, suddenly, another set of clues.

He pursued his idea feverishly.

And the pattern took shape!

CHAPTER 12

LORD SIMON QUINSEY

'And that's the position, Lord Simon.'

The First Officer looked hopefully across at Quinsey who, arrayed in a brocaded smoking-jacket, still leaned back in his chair, eyes closed, his sleek hair shining in the light which wavered as the ship slowly rolled from side to side. Everything in the cabin about him betrayed the man of taste and immense wealth: the pile of rare books in mellow calf bindings; the dark red roses in a square antique bronze vase; on the table at his elbow, an exquisitely carved jade cigarette box and a decanter of priceless brandy.

Quinsey opened his eyes lazily at last. 'So,' he said in his hesitating, curiously husky voice. 'The criminal remains at large. Murder stalks the *Florabunda*. You can't blame your passengers for being nervy. It's a bit disconcerting, what?'

'Aye. More than a bit.'

'And the longer I listen to you, the less able I am to guess who's guilty. Oh, don't think I am impugning your recital; you are admirably lucid. But the situation is not. Have some more brandy.'

Mr Waggish held his glass out. 'Well,' he said philosophically, 'if this is investigation, it's better than standing the dog watch at any rate.'

Quinsey grinned. '*Ad cratera per corpora*, what? I suspect you're secretly enjoying the whole bally thing.'

The First Officer laughed, a little embarrassed. 'I won't deny that,' he said slowly. 'It's the most interesting experience I've ever had – like a novel, so to speak. Very – well, psychological. The things that come out about human nature! For instance, who would have thought a lady like Mrs Chip-

Ebberly would be a smuggler? And then too, watching the great minds at work – very educational. And the suspense of wondering who the killer is – why, it is . . . it is . . .' Mr Waggish waved his hand vaguely, in indication that the Pleasures of Detection were somehow ineffable, and rolled a drop of brandy luxuriously on his tongue.

'I know.' A fleeting melancholy crossed Quinsey's long face. 'I know. *Et ego in Arcadia*, Mr Waggish.'

The First Officer responded to the nostalgia of the tone, though the words eluded him. He leaned forward eagerly. 'You wouldn't care to change your mind and step in after all, Lord Simon?' Quinsey adjusted his monocle severely. 'No, no. Definitely not my cup of tea.' Instinctively his fingers went out to stroke the Tennyson by his side: the cover had fallen back and hung down with its plate, engraved with the crest of his ducal family – a domestic cat crouched as to spring – and its motto: 'Lest Quinsey take me.'

'There is such variety,' Mr Waggish went on. 'Mr Poireau says it's a sense of order that makes for success in being a detective, Mr Bludgeon says it's guts, Sir Jon. will have it it's knowing Greek and Latin, whilst Mr Tourneur's all for being a gent. Which – well, which *trait* do *you* think is most important, Lord Simon?'

'Oh, rather; they're all indispensable prerequisites,' Quinsey said. He spoke a little vaguely, for his mind was on the *Idylls of the King;* but as his guest's blue eyes flew round-open in startled respect, he realized that he had, unawares, toppled over Mr Waggish's previous boundaries and opened up new vistas to him. Amused, he continued more attentively. 'At one time I should have said that, in addition to all that, there must be a certain *je ne sais quoi* – the nameless graces which no Watsons know, what?'

'The nameless – I expect that's a quotation?'

'Er – well, in part, don't you know.'

Mr Waggish nodded thoughtfully. 'I know about Watson . . . Sir Arthur Conan Doyle,' he informed Quinsey. 'But – you said, "at one time"? What would you say now, Lord Simon?'

Quinsey hesitated. Could one explain to this essentially artless officer the changes which had taken place since those 'years of *l'entre deux guerres*' when Lord Simon Quinsey, dazzling two continents with his birth, his wealth, his charm and wit, his distinction in a hundred fields, had yet been known best of all as amateur of crime? No; there was no explaining to the layman – in either subject – how he had risen from mysteries to Mystery . . . He said lightly, 'It's a long time since I gave it all up.'

'You were the greatest detective of all, they say.'

'Great Scott, Waggish! Blushes, modest, spare if possible. You've plenty of better brains at your service.'

'Ah, they're all grand men, and Miss Sliver's a very clever lady, but things want to be pulled together.'

Quinsey laughed. 'That's *your* job, old thing. You're the Master of Ceremonies, the *raisonneur*, and so on. Thou the first beams of Reason's scattered light must like a burning-glass unite.' As a question shaped itself on Mr Waggish's transparent countenance he appended hastily: 'Yes, a quotation; Cowley, but not inspired. Forget and forgive if possible. Sorry.'

At last the First Officer put his glass down and got up with some reluctance. 'Good night, Lord Simon. At any rate, if anything should occur to you, you'll – '

'Oh,' Quinsey promised, 'never fear. If the great brain hits upon the solution during sleep, or in our bath, we will let you know. Cheerio!'

Alone, Quinsey stared thoughtfully into his brandy-glass. He knew all the details of the *Florabunda* investigations, but he felt no inclination to join the chase. The old enchantment had fallen from the air. The men and women were crude as Punch and Judy, only for those two narrow words which shed interest upon them: *Who killed* . . . No one, surely, but an incorrigible *ingénu* like the First Officer would find them complex or mystifying. Nevertheless, Quinsey was irked by the existence of an unsolved probelm, and when his manservant came in he demanded:

'I dare say you're kept abreast of the ship's mystery, Punter. Have you any favourites? Whom are you backing?'

Punter, deftly laying out mauve silk pyjamas, coughed delicately. 'I am undecided, my lord. I have observed that Mr Homer Anderson's sartorial appointments are regrettable, even when due allowance is made for trans-atlantic taste and for the notorious laxity of shipboard life.'

'All too true. I too have seen and deplored. But sad experience teaches that virtue too often patronizes the Ninety-Shilling Tailors, whilst vice revels in Savile Row.'

'Quite so, my lord.'

'Then you have no theories about the case?'

'I should call it "baffling", my lord, if the word is not too hackneyed in the context.'

'I fear it is inescapable in the context, Punter. You retain your gift for the *mot juste*. I was at Eton and Balliol and I could not find a better.'

'Thank you, my lord. Will anything further be required?'

'No, nothing. Good night, Punter.'

'Good night, my lord.'

The mystery was strenuously recalled to Quinsey's attention next day when he came upon the four principal suspects – Anderson, Mrs Chip-Ebberly, Winifred Price, and Miss Despana – together in the Lounge, bristling with mutual suspicion like the characters in *The Critic* who end up pointing swords at one another's throats, so deperately entangled that none of them can move. Homer T. Anderson, in a costume which bore out Punter's severest strictures, was brandishing a book. At the sight of it Quinsey paused, his long eyes narrowing, and, hands in pockets, ambled unobstrusively nearer.

Anderson shook the book with a menacing grunt. 'It belongs to *someone*, I tell you!'

Winifred Price scowled. Her short dark hair was windblown, and there was a heavy jacket slung across her shoulders as if she had just come in from deck. 'Nobody can see the title when you wave it like that, Mr Anderson; but, whatever it is, it doesn't belong to me! And why do you care whose book it is?'

'The detectives say the killer is someone who thinks he's a cat. He's cracked, see? and thinks he's a cat. Well, there's a *picture* of a cat pasted inside this cover!'

'Oh!' ejaculated Mrs Chip-Ebberly.

It was the first time Quinsey had seen the noble lady since the exposé of her scheme to bilk Her Majesty's Government of a small fortune in precious stones. Her demeanour was unaltered; the line of her rugs was if anything more lumpish than before; Quinsey inferred that her strategy was to be that of the ostrich: since *she* had merely 'forgotten' about having the necklace with her, others must also have forgotten – leaving her free still to fix them with a thrilling scorn. She bent to look at the bookplate Anderson was exhibiting. 'But that is – '

Dolores Despana ostentatiously retreated several paces, one hand clutching her lovely throat. '*Yours!* I knew it!'

'It is no more mine than yours, Miss Despana.'

'Mine! I don't have any books. I never even *read* them!'

'One has not made the mistake of supposing that you did.'

Miss Despana was impervious to such a thrust, but Winifred Price suddenly giggled. Mrs Chip-Ebberly went oh, with the air of one driven to reckless lengths by sheer moral exasperation: 'As for all this nonsense about *Cats* – what sort of *codes* and *passwords* your organization may have chosen to employ, I do not pretend to know. But let me warn you once and for all: *Do not think that the Foreign Office is blind to your designs!*'

Miss Despana stared at her with uneasiness in her eyes. Anderson's bizarrely constructed features gave every indication of bewilderment. Winifred Price let out a second giggle. Her hand went nervously to her mouth, then to her roughened hair; she trembled. It looked like the onset of a good bout of hysterics, and Quinsey judged that the time had come to intervene. He advanced, one hand to his monocle.

'Oh, I say,' he asked innocently. 'Is that my book?' He held out his hand.

Anderson's triangular eyes lit up with triumph. 'Get the police!' he shouted. 'I mean, get the First Mate! Quick! We've got the killer.'

'*Honestly*, Mr Anderson!' Winifred Price, regaining her poise, viewed him with contempt.

Mrs Chip-Ebberly said tautly: 'That is *Lord Simon Quinsey!*'

'Help! Here's the murderer!'

'Don't be an ass, sir,' said Quinsey sharply as the bellow was repeated. 'Lower your voice, and have the goodness to return my property.'

Anderson took a step towards him, grunting. He towered over Quinsey. Reaching out to grab him with two moist and purply hands, he found his wrists caught in a steely grip, amazing in so slight an adversary, and was flung away with such force that he staggered against a bulkhead.

Quinsey dusted off his hands with a handkerchief, and flung the handkerchief away. 'And now, sir,' he demanded imperiously, 'how did you come upon this book?'

Anderson, choking with rage and excitement, glared at him sullenly: but he yielded to superior muscle and to a deeper force – the note of sixteen generations of feudal privilege and authority in Lord Simon's voice. 'It was there on the table, open. I saw the cat, so naturally I thought – ' A new expression traversed his face. 'Ha! if you didn't put it there I know who did!' He jabbed his forefinger towards Winifred Price vindictively. '*Her* boyfriend was standing right there by the table, and he went away when he saw me come in!'

'That's right, the Purser! I saw him, too.' Miss Despana's corroboration was enforced by a little gasp and a look which might have melted a man without Quinsey's long and varied experience of women.

He eyed her and Anderson with glacial appraisal. 'Very well,' he said curtly, 'The First Officer shall be informed of all this.'

Anderson beat an inglorious retreat, and Miss Despana followed. It was Bottom attended by a Titania with method in her dotage, Quinsey thought. Flinging a crocheted shawl about her in a quite swashbuckling manner, Mrs Chip-Ebberly stalked them from the room.

Tucking the book under his arm, Quinsey smiled down at Winifred. 'You don't think this brands me the villain, Miss Price?'

'Of course not! You're a detective.'

He chuckled. 'You make it sound like Cowboys and Indians,' he said happily. 'The good ones and the bad ones.' But, recognizing a wounded pride in her quick upward look, he added contritely: 'I say, forgive me – beastly rude. I didn't really mean that you're over-simplifying things. That would be unpardonable. Like telling someone in my generation he didn't have a sense of humour.' He smiled at her in whimsical distress. 'Anyway, the simple answer is the right one this time. I'm as pure as the driven snow, as far as the murder goes, I mean; and I shall take this book to Mr Waggish immediately. Or rather, if you'll do me the honour, I'll take it to him as soon as we have had some tea. Steward, take ours over to that corner.'

Winifred Price, cradling the cup in her hands, bent her pretty eyebrows in an attempt at practicality. 'Mrs Chip-Ebberly acted strangely when she saw your book.'

'Yes, I saw. But I think I know why. She recognized my crest – friend of the family, don't you see.'

'I know what you're thinking – that the *Purser* took your book and put it there! But you're absolutely wrong!'

'As a matter of fact, I hadn't supposed anything of the sort, particularly.' He looked at her curiously. 'But I'd rather like to know just why you think I *should* suppose so.'

'But you heard what Mr Anderson was insinuating! Everyone thinks – It's too silly! They think the Purser killed my uncle so he could marry me. They think we're in *love* with each other.'

'And that's just silly?' A certain camaraderie relieved Quinsey's question of offence.

'Yes, it is! I've never seen anything like the gossip on this ship. Because Tom and I *talked* together now and then, they think we must be having some Great Romance. Even though they *know* I'm engaged to Llewelyn!' Before Quinsey's look of steady amiability she blushed and bit her lip. 'Naturally, with propinquity, and being the same age and so on, naturally there has been a certain *physical attraction*.' Quinsey was interested in this shift from one code of proprieties to another: he resisted a wicked impulse to take her up at her own implications as she went on to appeal to the *savoir-faire* of a celebrated man of the world: 'Of course, it was understood that it was just a game. After all, I'm going to marry Llewelyn.'

'You're sure the *Purser* understands the exact nature of this – acquaintanceship? You women don't always know your own power, you know. I'd hate to think of your playing ducks and drakes with the poor blighter's affections!'

'Certainly. He has a girl in Manchester. Anyone he meets on board, like me, just represents a temporary transference of attachment, more or less unconscious.'

'I see. . . . I may say, if it's not too fearfully impertinent, that it's just as well. He's a delightful chap and all that, but a bit apt to fly off the handle, what?'

'Fly off the handle! Good heavens,' said Winifred Price with a pedantic composure that left his lordship breathless, 'He's fundamentally unstable, anyone can see that. I'm afraid he's *immature*. In fact, before he marries that girl he ought *really* to put himself into the hands of a *really competent* psychiatrist.'

And, thought Quinsey with relief and a sense of his own advancing years, I *think* she means it: no contamination by essence of sour grape. . . . He said with a twinkle: 'That's that, then. But it's thoroughly unorthodox of you, Miss Winifred. Every well-conducted murder mystery is supposed to end up with the marriageable characters paired off neatly.'

'I know!' she laughed back. 'Do you think, I should stage a great farewell scene on the bridge, with the passengers for audience?'

'With music from *Pinafore*? A beautiful thought.'

Her face sobered and she asked abruptly: 'You said – *end up*?'

'I didn't mean that I see the end of it.'

She sighed. 'What does it all mean, Lord Simon? The murder, and attacks, and smuggling plots, and things you can't even give a name to, like the – well, stealing your book. What was *that*?'

'It was the cat,' Quinsey retorted irrepressibly. Miss Price, who had less intuitive recognition of quotation than Mr Waggish, looked blank. He said more seriously, 'A killer with a cat complex does seem a bit thick.'

'Oh, but the cat is a very common symbol, modern psychology has found! Sexual – female,' she explained conscientiously. 'Modern psychology has discovered how people *do* have these strange obsessions. How they think they're God, or have aeroplane engines inside them, or – '

'Or that they're made of glass and will break if anyone comes near, or that jolly chap in Galen who thought the world was resting on his shoulders?' Quinsey suggested glibly. 'Modern psychology is a splended thing.'

'When I asked Mallory King, he said he'd begun to think it is a *Cheshire* cat, whatever *that* may mean!'

Quinsey was startled. With a sign for the deficiencies of

progressive education he told her: 'Even if you scientists can't spare much time for stories, Miss Winifred, you ought to look that one up; the Cheshire Cat fancied himself as an authority in your own field, interested in deviations and so on. And another thing about that charming animal,' Quinsey added thoughtfully, 'he disappeared, leaving only a grin behind.'

After searching the part of the ship open to passengers, without success, Quinsey made an illegal sally into the Officers' Mess and found Mr Waggish consuming a hurried sandwich and a cup of tea. He recounted the latest incident. 'Oddly enough,' he concluded, producing the book, 'it belongs to *me*.'

Mr Waggish drained his cup and put it down. 'I know,' he said quietly.

Quinsey looked at him in some surprise.

'I noticed it in your cabin last night, Lord Simon. Well, not this very book, perhaps, but it was surely the same picture.'

'Did you, by Jove! And you didn't leap to the conclusion that I am the feline felon?'

'No,' Mr Waggish said simply. He got up, sighing. 'I suppose I must try to find out who took it from your cabin.'

'Waste of time. Anyone could have done. But,' Quinsey offered as they mounted to A-deck, 'the egregious Anderson intimates that if I am not responsible for flaunting this particular avatar of the Cat, the *Purser* is.

'Now why would Tom do that? He has a bit of a temper, aye.' (Quinsey, remembering the instances he had heard of that temper, considered this a meiosis, but in deference to the peculiar mores of the British Merchant Navy he refrained from comment.) 'And you might say he's dotty over the lasses. But can you fancy him thinking he is a *Super-cat?*'

'In fact, a Tom-cat?' Quinsey took advantage of the First Officer's condition, in which speech was choked by the struggle between delight at this mild witticism and consternation at the off-chance that it was intended seriously, to take his departure.

'You must be mad,' he chanted to himself as he went, 'or you wouldn't have come here. We're all mad here. I'm mad. You're mad' It would have been unkind to inflict this echo of the Cheshire Cat upon the First Officer's sensibilities: yet it would scarcely be surprising, thought Quinsey as he entered his cabin, to see the toothy grin of that enigmatic animal suspended in the foggy middle distance somewhere off the port bow. This case passed all humours; it would not suit Miss Price's mentors, but, reflecting on its various ramifications, he wondered if the only recourse for the law-abiding voyagers on the *Florabunda* might not be a pious appeal to St Dympna, a saint perhaps not widely known, but who is duly reverenced within the Church of England as patron of those whose wits have gone astray.

Lord Simon belted a coat about him and went out on deck; tramping in the raw fog, he whistled with his customary taste and correctness, a few themes from Bach, Purcell, and Clementi, and pondered a few arresting facts:

Paul Price was a loss to no one. His body was found on deck. The cosh, the scarf, the pipe, the cheque, and the forgery had come into the hands of the investigators.

Quinsey was tantalized by something Mr Waggish had said the night before. Yes: each of the detectives aboard the *Florabunda* had followed, compulsively, his own bent, employed his own techniques: had found in this case that which he brought to it. As if manipulated by strings from above, Miss Sliver had knitted and drunk in confidences with hydroptic virtue, Mr King sought tropical significancies, Mr Beare engaged in a mode of dialectic, and Mr Bludgeon in a more visceral attack on the same problem. The same problem, but different in the mind of each . . . the Mind, that ocean where each kind doth streight its own resemblance find. . . . Quinsey mournfully shook his head as if to rid it of an inner fog micro-cosmically paralleling the moist pall which blotted sea and sky from view.

> I saw, that I saw not;
> Aye, and the Sunne which should teach mee, had forgot
> East, West, Day, Night . . .

The *Florabunda* curveted suddenly. An experienced sailor, Quinsey kept his sea-legs; but he did not see the little fountain-pen (dropped ten minutes ago by a careless passenger) which rolled under his foot. He slipped, staggered, and fell, and a sharp pain shot up and down his left leg.

'Blast!' muttered Lord Simon as the scorching pain increased. A slight nausea attacked him, though he did not lose consciousness; he was aware of the Purser luckily materializing out of nowhere and snapping his fingers as he shouted to some invisible menial for assistance; of Mrs Chip-Ebberly using her hands like long white flappers and declaring: 'This is too much! This is really *quite* too much!' Then, mercifully, Punter hastened up. There was a bad bit while they negotiated the trip below, but at last Quinsey was deposited on the settee in the Doctor's office.

The Doctor examined his ankle, clucking (it was the first quite professional sound Quinsey had ever heard him make), and ordered the room cleared – the Purser, Mrs Chip-Ebberly, Punter, and several miscellaneous passengers had pressed inside.

'Who pushed you, Lord Simon?'

Quinsey gritted his teeth against the pain. 'No one. Not a chance. I was damn' clumsy, that's all, the perfect lubber. What is it – a fracture?'

'No, no.' The Doctor crossed over to a cabinet. 'Just a sprain. And a good thing too,' he added rather huffily. 'I've never had so many things go wrong on a crossing: that journalist getting killed, Woodbin falling down, Miss Despana getting pushed and then getting a nose-bleed, and that lunatic attacking *me*, and now your ankle – '

'Sorry.'

The Doctor pulled down a roll of surgical gauze, wincing a little as he used the arm which had been damaged in his encounter with Mr Bludgeon, and began to unwind it. 'That's all right,' he said more graciously, 'so long as you weren't killed. I shouldn't want to have to do another post-mortem. How I'm supposed to get any writing done as it is, I cannot imagine.'

Quinsey, reduced to a – for him – almost unprecedented state of speechlessness, watched the bandaging.

'How's that?' The Doctor stepped back and regarded his handiwork proudly, his head cocked to one side.

'Aside from its hurting like billy-o, and preventing me from taking a step,' Quinsey retorted, 'it's doing nicely, thank you.'

'Oh – does it hurt? I'll give you something for that.' The Doctor went back to the cabinet and inspected a row of bottles. 'Let me see, let me see, something soothing,' he murmured. Seeing him touch first one, then another, and finally take down a third and read the label doubtfully, with his tongue sticking out between his teeth, Quinsey wondered if he were about to be poisoned by the depravity or (equally effective if less culpable) the incompetence of his physician. He felt about for a phrase with which to cushion that admirable rule of thumb, *Never take drugs from a suspect in a murder case*. But the Doctor handed him a pill and a glass of water with such engaging simplicity that he swallowed docilely.

'Thanks very much.'

'Not at all,' said the Doctor politely; he seemed to have been struck by a new idea. 'It's a pleasure, really. I've hoped to have an opportunity to chat with you, Lord Simon. The First tells me you're a literary man.'

This is always an ominous conversational gambit. Quinsey said warily: 'Well, that is to say, I pick up *incunabula* now and again . . .'

'Would you be a *patron*, now?'

'A patron?'

'A nobleman', the Doctor explained enticingly, 'who in return for trifling financial assistance to great writers is immortalized in dedicatory epistles – '

'Oh, yes. Quite. The system had its points, no doubt, but I have the impression that it went out with the eighteenth century.'

The Doctor brushed this pedantic reminder aside cavalierly. 'You may wonder how I came to be a ship's Doctor, Lord Simon,' he began. ('No, no,' Quinsey interposed courteously.) 'Naturally, I *started out* my practice on shore. In Newcastle-upon-Tyne it was; in Gosforth. But it was no go! There were too many patients altogether. They would positively line up, and show me their arms and legs, and ask questions, and talk about symptoms, and want things done for them. It took the best hours of the day. In three years I produced no more than fifteen hundred lines! So I cut loose. Here I came, and here I am. And very nicely it's worked out in many respects; but of course there are still these interruptions.'

'The ocean must be uncommonly inspiring.' Quinsey tried to get up, but his ankle gave an excruciating twinge.

'Careful,' warned the Doctor, wagging his finger. 'You had best not try to move, Lord Simon, not with that pill in you; it would be most unwise.' He went to his desk and proceeded to shuffle his papers together; they were slithering madly about, so that Quinsey was reminded irresistibly of Sackville's ditty:

> For tho' the Muses should prove kind,
>   And fill our simple brain,
> Yet if rough Neptune rouze the wind,
>   To wave the azure main,
> Our paper, pen, and ink, and we
> Roll up and down our ships at sea,
>   With a fa, la, la, la, la.

A mammoth bundle of manuscript in his arms, the Doctor took a seat by Quinsey's side and asked: 'Perhaps you would like to hear my poem?'

Quinsey closed his eyes. The question had been perfunctory; the answer was predetermined. Generations of breeding: the blood of fifteen dukes and countless assorted lesser peers: Eton: Balliol: St James's: Mayfair: and, latterly, the ante-chambers of Lambeth Palace – these must triumph when put to the test. With quiet dignity, he replied that nothing could give him greater pleasure.

'Let me see, then. Yes – or, no; not yet. But perhaps after all – Well, I might begin here. There won't be time for all of it, you know, but perhaps on your return trip?' The Doctor cleared his throat and commenced his recitation:

'Nor was the noble Tippitop from their dread power secure . . .'

Quinsey listened with the bland blank face which had served his nation so well on the delicate occasions when the Foreign Office had called on him for aid – when the hint of a sneer or a yawn had meant disaster.

'Gazella heaved a heavy sigh and tossed a tristful tail.
"Never" (quoth she) "will – " '

'*Tail?*' Quinsey was jolted out of his imperturbability.

'I might explain that in this canto Gazella has been turned
into a fish. It is only a temporary metamorphosis, of course;
on the allegorical level it means – But I'll go into *that* aspect
later.

' "Never" (quoth she) "will wanton wiles nor coward
   threats avail,
Cursed though I be with gills, and fins, in scaly prison here,
To lure my pure and faithful heart from Tippitoppus
   dear." '

Quinsey beguiled some time in trying to determine whether
the rhythm had been influenced by the fortuitous pitch and
roll of the *Florabunda*. Could there be a correlation between
heavy swells and masculine ending? . . . He realized that the
Doctor had come to a break, and expected comment. 'Oh,
jolly fine,' he murmured. 'Most interesting texture.'

The Doctor nodded matter-of-factly and resumed:

'For lo! ev'n in her fishy guise Gazella peerless shone.
The briny populace, adoring, set her on a throne,
And in their artless piscine way adored her as she sate.
The cruel Shark forbore to kill, forgetting all his hate.
Each wat'ry kind did reverence: the hoar majestic Whale,
The temperamental Octopus, the Crab, the modest Snail,
The frail irresolute Jelly-fish, the Oyster taciturn,
Th'obsequious Eel, the Lobster shrewd, the – '

There was a knock, but the Doctor did not hear it. The door
opened to reveal the troubled face of Punter, which cleared
as he saw his master on the settee. The Doctor broke off his
catalogue, sensing an alien presence, and scowled. In a stern
voice he said, 'His lordship must be left in *absolute* quiet!'
Quinsey waved dismissively, and his servant withdrew.

The Doctor went on and on. The words must have been
engraved on his heart by now; Quinsey, observing the face,
aglow with foetal ecstasy, eyes closed – the hands, waving in

graceful arcs – thought of auto-hypnosis. Mr Waggish put his head in, saw the Doctor reciting in bardic majesty and Quinsey trapped, gave Quinsey a comprehending grin, and heartlessly withdrew without coming to his assistance. The interruption went entirely unnoticed by the poet, who was quite rapt. And Quinsey began to feel that he himself might run some danger of hypnosis by the undulating arms: even the Doctor's injured arm rose and fell rhythmically, sheathed in its dark uniform sleeve – slightly spattered with pipe-tobacco ash and bedizened with its surgeon's stripes of red and gold. . . .

Quinsey tried to cry out, but found his mouth breaking into an enormous yawn. 'Doctor!' he managed to articulate, but the Doctor chanted on, oblivious. Quinsey fell asleep to this heptametrical lullaby.

The sedative was powerful. He slept like a log till morning, and woke in his own cabin, hungry and brisk, with only a faint throbbing from the sore ankle, and a perfect recollection of what he had learned the night before. When he had drunk his early tea he leaned back against his pillows and announced, 'Punter, I have solved the mystery of Mr Price's murder.'

'Indeed, my lord. May I offer my respectful congratualtions?'

'Thank you, Punter. I suppose something must be done about it. Yes. You'd better buzz off, after you've laid out my togs, and get the others together. Ask them to meet – No: Mr Beare will not like to leave his cabin. Go to him first, with my compliments, and ask if we may all meet there. Then go to Mr Waggish and the rest. Ask if we can meet at – say – ten o'clock.'

'Very good, my lord. Will your lordship wear the light tweeds?'

'No. Sackcloth, I think.'

'My lord?'

'With a spot of ashes.'

PART THREE

CHAPTER 13

EXPLICATIONS

'Forgive me for barging into things like this,' Quinsey begged his colleagues. 'But last night I just happened to hit on something which — taken with what *you* have all discovered — clears up our mystery. I listened to the Doctor's poem, you see — '

'*All* of it?' an awed voice interrupted him.

'A good two hours' worth. Then merciful oblivion; I fancy the sedative he gave me was stronger than he intended. As for the poem itself — ' Quinsey shuddered lightly. 'We needn't go into that, I think. Oh let th'Iambick Muse revenge that wrong! But it did put me on to something jolly useful.'

He related what he had learned in the Doctor's cabin. 'The conclusion, of course, is obvious.'

It was. There was a moment of silence, of unanimous comprehension.

'It might be described', said someone, 'as a *flattering* murder.'

Miss Sliver coughed. 'Appalling!'

Quinsey resumed: 'I was handed this note just now, but I've not yet opened it; it is addressed to all of us.' He slit the envelope and read aloud:

'Miss Sliver, My Lord, and Gentlemen:

'I was born in Devon, of poor but honest parents who put me to sea when I was fifteen years of age. Applying myself diligently to my work, I satisfied my superior officers, did well before the Board of Trade, and rose steadily till I reached my present rank.

'I was only sixteen when I came upon the book which was

to influence my entire life – *The Adventures of Sherlock Holmes*, by Sir Arthur Conan Doyle. It overwhelmed me altogether. Nothing, I thought, could be so fine as the genuis of its hero. What was my joy and my excitement when I learned that there were other, *even greater detectives!* From that time on I laid out the better part of my pay on detective novels. At first, ignorant lad that I was, I dreaded the day when there would be no more left to read. But soon I learned that the supply was inexhaustible – that the number of such stories increases year by year! All that I could lay hold of, I read.

'On the surface, my life might seem to be a dull round of standing watch, checking cargo, hurricanes, and shipwrecks – in reality it held the thrills which only Miss Dorothy Sayers, Miss Christie, Mr Stout, etc., etc., can give. From them I learned about corpses, clues, Oriental poisons, slow-witted policemen, hermetically sealed death-chambers, forged wills, and snowed-in houseparties full of aristocratic people and beautiful girls. If I had dared express my dearest wish, it would have been for the opportunity – not to *outwit* one of my heroes, for that I knew was impossible – but to observe one of them at work.

'When I found that *nine detectives were actually aboard the Florabunda*, I knew that some higher Power, Providence as Miss Sliver would say, had stepped in to lend me a hand. And so I cast about for a suitable victim.

'The choice was not hard. I did not personally know Mr Price, as a matter of fact we never exchanged a word, and so far as I know he lived and died unaware of my existence, but I had many reasons for disapproving of him. He had no decent respect for the sea, the Ship, or the Captain. He insulted my friend and that fine gentleman, the Purser. He criticized the work of my talented friend and shipmate, the Doctor. He was a person of low moral character in general, and I knew he would be no loss.

'That settled – and once I had confiscated the weapon which a passenger carelessly left lying about – it was just a question of *time* and *place;* and I did not have long to wait. On the second night out, as the Doctor read to me during the Middle Watch, I felt inclined for some reason to stretch my legs, and knowing he would not mind a short absence, I popped down to the main deck. I saw Mr Price smoking at the rail, all alone, and realized that my chance had come. It was the work of a moment to hit him on the head, haul him over to a bulkhead, and stow him away under a tarpaulin, safe and sound. I rejoined the Doctor, and spent the next few hours listening to Tipptoppus and Gazella.

'Before turning in (it being by then about six bells) I thought I might take a look at the victim's cabin. On deck just inside his door lay an envelope with a cheque inside, and there was a page of his literary bilge in the typewriter. I added a few lines of my own, to fill up the blank space, thinking it might come in handy as a "red herring" (if I use the word rightly) later on. then I took the paper, the cheque, and the cosh away with me.

'I need not tell you that I did this for the same reason that I had stowed the pipe and scarf beneath the corpse. I knew that the crimes you investigate always have something odd about them, something "artistic" so to speak, to make them more interesting to the reader. This bothered me a great deal at first because I have never been a fanciful chap and could not think of an unusual touch, then I happened to see the scarf in a passageway just after hearing some passenger call Mr Price a "rat", and my mind flew to a book I had once glanced at in the Doctor's cabin whilst he recited to me. It was not convenient to borrow the Boatswain's pipe as I would have preferred, so I fetched a briar-pipe from the store, in hopes it would serve at a pinch, and carried it about with the muffler and the cosh till the time should come to use them.

'I never would have dreamed that they meant all those deep things that Mr King discovered in them with Gib the cat and so forth, and it was surely very fine to learn the explanation and find what I had really meant; but as far as that goes you were all even finer than I had hoped and I should like to say right now how grateful I am and what a privilege it has been to watch you.

'Well, everything went on very well, though I had to do such things as bring out the cheque and the cosh and the torn page, and later borrow Lord Simon's book, in order to persuade some of you to help, and also of course to add more Mystery.

'I had one problem you might call a "moral problem". Needless to say, I could not tell you everything I knew or there would not have been any mystery, but how far ought I to try to mislead you? Actually, it was not too hard to decide. It would not have been above-board to tell any downright lies. Besides, it would have been useless. After all, I have spent my life at sea, far from towns and cities and the gay world of sophisticated Society, where men learn to Mask and deceive and sail under False Colours day and night. Indeed when I thought of this I could hardly believe my own boldness in trying to keep any secret from you who in case after case see through the most clever, wicked, Hypocritical actors who build up perfect alibis and plan for their murders many weeks or possibly even many months beforehand. Surely I would be discovered straight off, and the whole point of my murder would be wasted!

'But luck, or should I more rightly, as Miss Sliver would, say Providence, was with me. Once things got rolling I never really had to play a part, for many false clues opened up at once to distract attention from me. It was quite a pleasure, really, to see how well I had made my choice, as you brought Mr Price's true character to light. It was clear that many other people might very likely have done away with him. As you uncovered the truth about him and Miss Price and the other passengers I lost my bearings entirely; I became so confused that at times I wondered how even the greatest of detectives could steer a straight course through it all! But, believe me, my faith in you never *truly* faltered. I knew you would get to me in time.

'Once Lord Simon found out how the Doctor loses track entirely of what goes on about him whilst he recites his poem, I knew the end had come. Now that my alibi had capsized, all the other evidence against me would fall into line – the careless way I had sometimes let it slip that I knew more about you than I dared admit; how anxious I was to have you all lend a hand; how interested I was in your methods and your styles; also, lately, how anxious I have been to protect my shipmates from suspicion as you seemed to be closing in on them; for I admit that to those who do not know them as I do the Old Man and my friends the Purser and the Doctor might sometimes look suspicious, as they each have a special task, a "monomania" as some of you might call it, and how could I explain to you without ending the case too soon that it was not a monomaniac you should be looking for, but me?

'How I wish I could be there to hear you discuss the solution of the murder! But I know from my books that the legal technicalities that usually follow on your last chapters are a bore for everyone concerned, and also, and maybe more important, a ship's officer is responsible for "maintaining discipline and good order by his example, personal behaviour and character", and seeing a senior officer in the brig would not be good for the crew's morale, I think. And so I bid farewell for ever to my ship, my shipmates, home, and England, with no regrets:

'*To have seen such heroes walk the deck, I count the World Well lost!*

'With thanks and eternal admiration I remain,
Yours respectfully,
WM. WAGGISH, 1st Officer, R.M.S.*Florabunda*'

CHAPTER 14

POSTLUDE IN NEW YORK HARBOUR

As the doctor swung up the companion, the Second Officer tottered out of the bridge-house and hurried aft with a white, set face. A furious roar pursued him from within.

'What's biting the Old Man now?' the Doctor inquired of the Purser, who was leaning at the boat-deck rail, watching the last of the fog blow off.

The Purser shrugged as another roar came forth. 'Ah,' he said, 'you can't blame him if he's in a bad mood this afternoon. He's still all fouled up over those detectives. First when they thought the First had jumped overboard they wanted the ship turned round to hunt for the body. Then when they heard about the Number Six boat being gone they wanted him to radio ashore for search-planes to be sent out. . . . *Planes!* He wasn't half wild. Came near clapping them all in irons.'

'Ah!' The Doctor puffed on his pipe reflectively. 'Fancy Waggish bumping off that blighter,' he observed after a time. 'I never knew he took those books so seriously.'

'I thought he must have done, when he brought us those farewell notes last night.' The Purser's eye followed a small boat which was making for the *Florabunda* in a businesslike manner. 'But one didn't like to ask.'

'Where *is* that island of his, do you know?' asked the Doctor after another interval.

'He never said; it isn't on the charts. . . . Here comes the pilot.'

'It would be a fine quiet place to work, I dare say.' A

wistful look on the Doctor's face suddenly turned to one of real vexation. 'Damn it!' he said, as the true significance of the facts sank in. 'And I suppose he won't be coming back? Why, that means I can never read my Eleventh Canto to him!'

PANDORA WOMEN CRIME WRITERS

For further information about Pandora Press
Books, please write to the Mailing List Dept. at
Pandora Press, 11 New Fetter Lane, London
EC4P 4EE.

GREEN FOR DANGER

by Christianna Brand

This is Christianna Brand's most celebrated
novel of crime and detection. In the brilliant
light of an operating theatre, during London's
war-time blitz, the patient is murdered – a
harmless old postman. And one of the six
members of the theatre staff must be the
murderer. Soon the whole hospital seethes with
mystery. A nurse, creeping back to the theatre
at dead of night in search of a clue encounters
a masked figure with surgical scalpel raised.
The tap of an unlit gas fire is turned on. Tablets
of morphine disappear. *Green for Danger* was
the basis for the film of the same name.

Pandora Women Crime Writers
May: LC8: 160pp
0–86358–208–7: paperback

DEATH OF A DOLL

by Hilda Lawrence

High tension pervades this whodunnit set in a
girls' hostel in America. A murder takes place
in this claustrophobic all-female environment,
and the classic female detection process is
set in motion to solve it. Hilda Lawrence is well
known to aficionados of crime fiction, as the
author of *The Pavillion* and other excellent
novels. *Death of a Doll* is unusual in having no
single central narrator. It is also one of her finest
novels.

Pandora Women Crime Writers
May: LC8: 232pp
Paperback: 0–86358–205–2: paperback

AMATEUR CITY

by Katherine V. Forrest

A modern whodunnit, in the best traditions of
the genre.
' "Please look at me Miss O'Neil." Kate Delafield
sat with arms crossed, elbows resting on the
table. Her light blue eyes were not cold they
were not hostile, but they bored into Ellen's as
if she were seeing all the way to the back of
her head. "There was a reason why a murderer
got across that hallway to safety, why you never
saw who it was" '
Kate Delafield, tough leader of the homicide
investigation team, soon discovers strong
motives for the killing of Fergus Parker in an
office united in its hatred of him. Her own
personal life is in crisis, and she finds her path
increasingly intersecting with that of chief
witness, Ellen O'Neil . . .

Pandora Women Crime Writers
May: LC8: 232pp
Paperback: 0–86358–200–1: paperback